A Flight to A Story

This Point in Time
נקודת הזמן הזאת

By J.W. Krych
Forgiveness is Universal
הסליחה היא אוניברסלית

Copyright © 2018 James W. Krych

All rights reserved.

ISBN: 9781791785529

Cover Art and Design by Ranka Stevic

Based on the characters and books by L. Frank Baum and Ruth Plumly Thompson

Illustrations By:
Chiara Civati

This is a work of fiction. Names, characters, businesses, places, events and incidents are either the products of the author's imagination or used in a fictitious manner. Any resemblance to actual persons, living or dead, or actual events is purely coincidental.

DEDICATION

Am Yisrael Chai!

Sh'ma Yisrael Adonai Eloheinu Adonai Echad

J.W. Krych
Winter A.D. 2018

ACKNOWLEDGMENTS

I am deeply indebted to the enormous amount of technical, cultural, and historical help I had during this project. I simply cannot list all of it but the following were major sources for me. To all of you, Todah Rabah!

Radio:

John M. Hoyt

Morris B. Cohen, Ph.D.
Assistant Professor, Electrical and Computer Engineering
Georgia Institute of Technology
LF Radio Lab

Kurt Diedrich

Space and Lunar Base:

Scott Manley
Winchell Chung and his Atomic Rockets website
Theodore W. Hall
Isaac Arthur

Hebrew Transliteration:

Lenah Grogan
Jewish Forums at The Hebrew Cafe
www.qbible.com

Civil Engineering:

Burke Rawson

ACKNOWLEDGMENTS(CONTINUED)

Hebrew Date Converter:
https://www.hebcal.com/converter/

Holocaust Survivor Resources:
Lenah Grogan
Esther Vivien Levy

Information on the Holocaust:
United States Holocaust Memorial Museum

Palmach:
Jewish Virtual Library
Tablet Brothers-and-sisters-in arms by Tal Kra-Oz August 26th, 2015

A shout out to the tilapia farming company that wished to remain anonymous.

Finally, to Nikki Rae for her editing and Ron Baxley Jr. and Erica Olivera for their feedback.

CONTENTS

Acknowledgments

The Gardener

5th of Adar 5805 (22 FEB 2045)	16
6th of Adar 5805 (23 FEB 2045)	52
7th of Adar 5805 (24 FEB 2045)	75
8th of Adar 5805 (25 FEB 2045)	95
9th of Adar 5805 (26 FEB 2045)	121
10th of Adar 5805 (27 FEB 2045)	153
14th of Iyar 5807 (Epilogue)	174

Version 1.2   11 MAY 19

THE GARDENER

In a most unusual location, planted at one of the most inhospitable regions known to mankind, a little plot of the Garden of Eden had been recreated. In the very middle of the garden were three pairs of date palms, Abraham/Sarah, Isaac/Rebecca, and Jacob/Rachel – descendants of the Judean Date Palm named Methuselah.

Stationed underground, based at Tsiolkovsky Crater on the far side of the moon, it was rectangular in shape with a curved ceiling. Off to the side were three compartments—rooms—which housed the "real" business for which the garden had been designed; two were for vertical gardening and the last was for aquaculture. The vertical gardening compartments each housed several panels on which plants were grown and LED and fiber-optic lights provided the needed illumination. Finally, the aquaculture compartment contained a large pool which held tilapia, a kosher fish. And to feed them were basins of duckweed housed in two columns.

Overlooking its little ponds here and there, the grapevines, cherry shrubs, and dwarf trees—of which cherry and plum were included—and several electric grills and a faux stone fire pit, was the curved ceiling with a too-good-to-be-true feature: a high-definition display made up of roll-able LED screens. With a suspended sun-globe and using soothing fiber-optic provided light, the ceiling could provide breathtaking night and day views of anywhere in Israel. These would also be previously recorded or streamed from several locations in Israel itself.

Though not technically kept as a secret, knowledge of its existence was limited to the various crews that had manned the station and to the friendly space-faring nations that had been given an opportunity to visit – especially after a long voyage. And delightful shock at what the Israelis had accomplished was always expressed.

In reality, this should not have come as a surprise, for the Jews of Israel had made the deserts bloom back on earth and what is the moon but an airless desert?

However, there were a few more steps that had to be taken before this patch of lunar soil was turned into a small piece of Eden.

Initially, it *was* a well-kept secret. When the Israeli Space Agency (ISA) had announced its intentions to build a radio observatory base and locate it at Tsiolkovsky Crater; they had given the international scientific community no less than four artists' conceptions of Base Esther. However, once construction had begun in the late summer of 2030, the actual base, for security's sake, was nothing like it had been portrayed. In fact, the garden's plans were never mentioned.

It was only after all other construction had been completed that work on the garden commenced in earnest. First, an extremely large inflatable structure was placed at the exact location where the garden would eventually stand. Then automated construction diggers were run around the clock to excavate the site. The excess lunar regolith, the layer of deposits on the surface, and the underlying material were then added to the berms around the landing pads one kilometer away.

Once the target depth had been achieved, construction crews excavated a tunnel to the base and installed a multi-stage airlock. This prevented lunar dust from contaminating the air, for lunar dust is quite abrasive and is a hazard to the lungs and eyes. They next dug out where the three extra compartments would be located.

Finally, the crews lowered the inflatable structure. The Chief Civil Engineer of the project, Yonatin Rawsonson, conducted load and soil bearing tests to calculate the footers needed to handle the weight of the structure. With the footers in place, it was time for the next step: strengthening the structure.

Wire mesh was first planted throughout the interior. Next, ribs manufactured from lunar titanium were connected and then anchored to the footers. Finally, the inside was filled with a type of lunar concrete, using lunar dust, water from lunar ice, a powdered resin, and synthetic fibers. Once all of that had been hardened and cured, the roof was backfilled with lunar soil and made flush to the surface – a depth of about five meters. This would protect the garden from radiation and micrometeorites.

Work then commenced on readying the three compartments. This included installing the water lines, electrical, fiber optic cables, and ventilation. As the vertical gardening and aquaculture began, the most important step in creating the garden was implemented: preparing the lunar soil.

By itself, lunar soil cannot be used to grow crops because the needed nutrients are locked up in tough minerals. However, in an experiment conducted by NASA, it was found that the addition of cyanobacteria—originally found in hot springs in Yellowstone National Park—along with water, air, and light produced acids that broke down the tough minerals.

Section by section, the lunar soil was dug up and placed into tanks where the cyanobacteria worked its magic. Thus when each batch was deemed ready for the next step, the now-processed soil was placed into another tank where a source of nitrogen was added – which was readily available from the base and construction crews.

As the soil for the garden was prepared, the interior of the structure was sprayed with a specially-designed type of water-proof insulation that would hide the wire mesh. At the same time, the three pairs of Judean Date Palms were transferred over from Base Netanyahu in pots –

already two years old by that time. Finally, the roll-able displays were attached to the ceiling and turned on to provide both daytime and nighttime scenes. The crews installed the sun-globe and numerous speakers for future ambiance.

For the time being, the displays projected only onto an empty field, for which the speakers were but silent witnesses. Had one only viewed the soil, they could have imagined it was from Israel or even from Kansas! However, it was entirely on the moon and ready for planting.

The plants wouldn't be safe for consumption by the base personnel – not yet. The reason for this was quite simple: lunar soil contained an abundance of heavy metals.

In large concentrations, this could be quite dangerous to humans. Common heavy metals included barium, arsenic, chromium, cadmium, mercury, lead, silver, and selenium. The trick then would be to remove these hazardous materials before anyone tried to eat any of the plants grown here.

Fortunately, there was a low-tech solution readily available to solve the problem. The answer was to use something called phyto-remediation. Certain plants had an ability to concentrate the heavy metals and literally do the dirty work of cleaning the soil.

For the first year, the phyto-remediation processes relied on Indian Mustard Greens and after seven weeks they would be harvested and placed into air-tight containers. The soil would be plowed and another crop begun. In total, seven crops were produced, placed into the containers, and then sent to a smelter.

Finally, the on-site botanists utilized a plant known to be a hyperaccumulator to slurp up everything else that could have been left behind. That plant was the *Salix Viminalis*, otherwise known as the osier willow or the basket willow. The soil was temporally made wetter than normal for the willows as they grew and performed their phyto-remediation. After a year of growth and extensive testing for heavy metals, the willows too were harvested, removed, and sent to the smelter.

At long last, the garden was ready and the three pairs of Judean Date Palms were the first transplanted, followed by grapevines, shrubs, dwarf trees, and many others. Then, all that was needed was time as everything grew and matured at different intervals.

As the seasons went by each year, the transition would bring a different crew to maintain the garden. Over time, the need for a support staff diminished with each crew iteration until only one chief botanist—listed on the crew roster as "The Gardener"—was permanently assigned.

Chatulah

It was late afternoon of the 23rd of Sh'vat, 5805, which in the Gregorian Calendar meant February 10th, 2045. The garden was still, the ambiance turned off for the day. The overhead displays presented an incredibly breathtaking view across the Sea of Galilee, towards the skyline of Tiberius, from the cliffs of the Southern Golan Heights.

There was only one person in the entire garden at the time: a woman in a light blue jumpsuit wearing tennis shoes, zipping around using a push-reel mower. The mower was an ideal tool for garden upkeep; it was pollution free, didn't need electricity, the clippings provided a free source of fertilizer for the remaining grass, and as a bonus it offered a great cardio workout. It was also nearly silent, only the *snip-snip-snip* of the blades indicating the machine was working.

After a few more minutes, she finished mowing with a customary hard sprint. Then, after returning the mower to a storage shed and having a pleasant cool-down, she began her weight lifting at the resistance training station - which also had a nearby treadmill for normal cardiovascular exercise. Everyone at the base had to conduct two hours of daily exercise: one for the heart and one for the muscles. It was a major way to stay healthy while residing in the reduced gravity of the moon.

She commenced her lifting regime with gusto. She was a thin woman, but by no means frail; she had an athletic build due to exercise and great genes which included a Romani great-grandmother. Her eyes and hair were brown with her coiffure long and wavy. Her nickname was Chatulah, Hebrew for a female cat, though truth be told, the Hebrew for date palms better attested to her real name.

She was the oldest of five children, the tie-breaker when it came to boys and girls, and her 45th birthday was only three weeks away. In all of her family, she was the favorite of her great-grandmother because she had hung onto every word of the heroic stories of fighting in the Palmach during the Israeli War of Independence. With tears, she had quietly hearkened to her great-grandmother's recollections of traveling through Europe after she had been liberated from Auschwitz.

Chatulah was also the only relative that ever believed the fantastical tale of how her great-grandmother's people came to wander through the countries of Southern Europe.

Shortly after high school, Chatulah joined the Caracal Battalion of the Israel Defense Forces to honor her great-grandmother's memory. She continued to do so after the mandatory 26 months of service, as a reservist, finally becoming an officer after attending Bahad 1 at Camp Laskow.

She had come from a family of farmers, so it was only natural that she would earn a Bachelor's and Master's Degree of Science in Agriculture from Hebrew University – concluding with a PhD. Outside of Reserve Duty, she would divide her time at her family's farm and any one of several kibbutzim – communal settlements – her favorites being Kfar Masaryk and Kibbutz Sasa.

She hadn't been the first of her family to go into space. That honor went to one of her brothers. Once she had listened to his own experiences in orbit and on the moon, she felt wanderlust to explore. Fortunately, Base Netanyahu and its lunar agricultural center needed experienced botanists and after training with the ISA, she was part of the crew there, gaining vital hands-on experience that in time would enable her to volunteer for duty at Base Esther.

Buzz! The alarm announced that her hour of weight training was over. Smiling at the feeling of having had a great workout, she stretched. Then, grabbing her towel and a cold grapefruit-flavored sparkling water, she ran towards a three-meter tall platform that oversaw the entire garden. With a powerful jump, Chatulah took advantage of the 1/6th gravity and leaped up to the top with a single bound and landed deftly on her feet.

Sipping her water, she was reflective as she looked out over the entire garden. She smiled yet sighed, for not only had the garden been fruitful, but it had multiplied its bounty much more than normal. This was a problem. Normally she'd only need herself to handle each harvest, but not this time. Everything would be ripening close to Purim and her birthday, and with the yearly station audits, no help could be spared.

Still, she blessed the harvest as it was a daily routine she'd had ever since she was a little girl working on her family's farm. *"Baruch atah Adonai Eloheinu Melech ha-olam borei pri ha-etz" Blessed art Thou, Lord our God, King of the universe who creates the fruit of the tree.*

Chatulah lifted her head and with a heavy heart, prayed for help. *"Elohim sheli ha pa bemitzi chazra" This time, Lord my God, this time I truly need help.*

A few more gulps of water and she was done. She jumped off the platform and landed on a patch of soft grass. Satisfied with everything in the garden, Chatulah headed towards the main compartments of Base Esther, bunny-hopping all the way.

Passing through the multi-stage airlock, she made a quick detour to her stateroom, which was about five meters away. Grabbing her evening clothes, toilet kit, and a pair of sandals, she continued to bunny-hop to the female washroom module. Once there with the door shut behind her, the dirty clothes were thrown into a container and she placed her clothes and kit on a nearby bench.

The module held four showers, three vacuum toilets with privacy stalls, three sinks with a large mirror, and a large hot water on-demand system. The male washroom module was identical and even though lunar ice was readily available, conservation was king to the efficiency of the base.

She swiped her ID badge as she stood up to a shower head. The system used her credentials from its database and prepared the temperature to her liking. Then she received a rinse that lasted 30 seconds. Quickly using her body wash, Chatulah pushed a little green button and 45 seconds of water rinsed everything down. The dirty water was already being sucked into the water recycling system.

Back in her stateroom, she rested on her part of the bunk bed. Normally, there would be another person sharing her quarters, but there currently wasn't a need. It was a rather spartan affair, too; other than a couple of desks that also had drawers for storing clothes, there was a small water closet with sink and several rods that held fresh jumpsuits. Of course, there was a base intercom with video, connections for her tablet or workstation, and a smart screen that was an alarm clock and played music or movies.

She prayed again, asking for help before she read her Tanakh (The Jewish Bible). It was a habit that her grandmother and mother had installed within her. Yawning, Chatulah set the book aside after only a few passages, prepared her blankets, and then walked up to retrieve a picture she hid behind one of her and her great-grandmother taken a year before she had passed.

The stories flowed through her heart as if she was still there at her great-grandmother's hospice bed. With all the craftiness of cats, she was told, they had to be while traveling after liberation. It was her great-grandmother who had bestowed on her the nickname Chatulah, and she gladly accepted it. Even after liberation, it wasn't safe, so her great-grandparents fled south until they were met by the miracle of miracles – The Jewish Brigade Group in Tarvisio, Italy.

It was in Tarvisio that they were taught how to fight with the weapons the Jewish Warriors possessed. Then they were transported south and loaded onto ships to be smuggled into what would soon be the restored state of Israel. Together, with her Jewish husband and many other brave souls, they fought for Israel's freedom.

Chatulah remembered her great-grandmother's plea to her as she unfolded the picture – the yellowish paper that revealed the One. Drawn when her great-grandmother was only eight years old, the very one that had sent her people from a magical land to the countries of Southern Europe. Her fingers grazed the figure, traced the long hair, the circlet, and finally stopped at the twin poppies the young girl wore. Chatulah sighed deeply but was determined. Somehow, someway, she would indeed carry out great-grandmother's wish.

"Chatulah, zichri zot ve-tinkemi et nikmati im ei paam ya'aleh be-yadech. Hayiti ha-yachid mimishpachti she-sarad et machanot ha-hashmadah. Hayinu tish'a bnei mishpachah k'she-yaradnu mi-kronot ha-bakar ha-amusim. Simnu li lifnot yamina, ve-ha-sh'ar hunchu lalechet smola la-miklachot.... At ha-yechida she-ma'amina li! Nikmi et nikmateinu!"

Chatulah, remember this and avenge me if you ever can. I was the only one of my family who survived the death camps. There were nine of us when we came out of those packed cattle cars. I was directed to go to the right, the rest were told to go left to the showers... You are the only one who believes me. Avenge us!

This Point in Time

"The gypsies she banished from Oz altogether, sending them by her magic to wander through the countries of Southern Europe." Ojo in Oz by Ruth Plumly Thompson 1933

5ᵀᴴ OF ADAR, 5805
(WEDNESDAY, 22 FEBRUARY 2045)

In the silence of space, the Bravo faithfully continued on its programmed path. In the cabin, Jonathan and Ozma were in the deepest of sleep, while far below a magnificent storm raged like a tempest. The piles of clouds burst forth numerous crackles of lightning —an awesome display of nature's might—and if the occupants had been awake, they would have been privy to such transient luminous events such as red sprites, elves, blue starters, blue and gigantic jets, and pixies. It would have been a most magical show!

Suddenly, the alarms of the Bravo rang out, rudely disturbing the sleep out of its occupants. "Object ahead!" the cockpit display announced as Jonathan, out of sheer instinct, reached over and tightened Ozma's straps. He quickly placed and locked her helmet on while she was still waking up, connected her air hoses, thrust her gloves at her, and secured the tablet - all in a matter of seconds and before he had donned his own gear.

It was then that they noticed the Object, and it was big enough to be seen without the use of any instruments. A sphere of about a mile across had manifested itself; the lights of numerous stars and galaxies reflected all about it like a darkened fishbowl.

Both glanced at the other. "What is that, Jonathan?" Ozma asked with apprehension in her voice.

He didn't answer as the Bravo's systems grabbed his immediate attention. The alarms and messages informed him that the Bravo's programmed course was directly guiding it towards the sphere. He gulped as he looked ahead at the ever-increasing size of the sphere as it filled the cockpit window. "I...I didn't think I'd ever see one of these.".

Ever closer did the Bravo and sphere approach each other. Ozma squeezed his hand.

"It's a wormhole, Ozma." Jonathan calmly informed her while masking his own fears. "It's also called an Einstein-Rosen bridge."

"A bridge? But to where?"

He glanced at her just before the Bravo touched the wormhole's surface.

Base Esther

Named after the famed, courageous Jewish Queen Esther, the ISA's Base Esther Radio Observatory utilized many hard-earned lessons in lunar construction. The greatest of which was cost and how to mitigate and manage it as much as possible.

The first step involved an extremely detailed mapping of the area – Tsiolkovsky Crater. Using this data, CAD (computer aided design), systems calculated numerous solutions for an optimal base. Everything that could be planned for, was, and this included where the fiber optic cables would be trenched.

Next, in-house facilities at Base Netanyahu commenced the 3-D printing of the individual modules: staterooms where the future personnel would sleep and rest, washrooms, laundry modules, medical modules, dining facility modules, and more. Most of them utilized a standardized layout to mitigate cost even further. Automated excavators were loaned to the project, of which the microwave sintering machines were vital; any asset that was refurbished to the point of being nearly brand-new would be incorporated.

Items that couldn't be built were slowly brought to the base for storage. A late decision to make part of the upcoming Base Esther an adjunct of Base Netanyahu, on the dark side of the moon, meant additional resources would be available – and they were rapidly acquired. Finally, construction began.

Monitored by civil engineering crews, automated excavators carried out their arranged tasks and when the proper depth had been achieved, the Chief Civil Engineer and his team conducted load and soil bearing tests in order to calculate the correct footers. For the adjunct station, this meant footers for four enormous inflatable structures – similar in shape to the one used for the Garden. The inflatable structure of Base Esther itself was similar to a geodesic dome with five passageways that branched off. The center would be the Communications Information Center (CIC): the brain of the base once the radio observatory commenced its scientific mission.

As each structure's lunar concrete cured, additional work was performed. For the adjunct station, this included two landing pads with sloping walls and berms. Base Esther received its assorted modules, each passageway with a specific function. There was the medical passageway with its clinic and MRI/portable X-Ray module. The longest passageway was the crew quarters with the washrooms and a backup life support module. The dining facility had its kitchen module on one side while several rectangular modules were linked together like building blocks to make the dining room and meeting room. There was the passageway with the laundry and water recycling module. Finally, the fifth passageway contained modules for servers, backup power fuel cells, main life support, and the main airlock that would also provide access to the train that connected Base Esther to the Adjunct Station. The eventual multi-stage airlock going to the Garden was placed near the entrance to the crew quarters.

Guided with precision, the trenches for the fiber optic cables, power lines, and their conduit were dug up and then covered over after everything had been laid down. All of this was accomplished remotely, monitored by various engineers, and each end was terminated by a junction box to where an instrumentation module would be connected.

As work continued on the interior sections of both Base Esther and the Adjunct, the automated excavators—including the microwave sintering machines—continued to prove their worth! Working as a team, the excavators created a main road starting from Base Esther that branched off to where each of the five Receiving Base Stations would be located.

In conjunction with a couple of "portable" reactors weighing in at around 250 tons, the microwave sintering machines utilized the unused electrical power to turn lunar dust into incredibly strong bricks. However, it was the ability to microwave the lunar material into ceramic sheets that made paved roads, base station pads, the and the sloped walls quite feasible. In a way, the microwave sintering machines worked in a similar fashion to the bulk asphalt paving machines back on earth.

There was a vital reason for all of this and it was to mitigate the effects of the extremely abrasive lunar dust on their supporting equipment. Indeed, when the Apollo 12 Lunar Module had landed only 183 meters from the Surveyor 3 unmanned craft, it was found to have had essentially sandblasted the probe with the lunar dust kicked up by the descent engine.

Once the pads of each base station were cool enough, it was time to install the instrumentation module. A special lunar truck delivered one to each site, laid it close to the junction box, and anchored it to the pad. To protect from lunar dust contamination, a temporary tent was placed around the module which allowed the technician to make the needed connections to the junction box. Once the module was tested on-site and remotely, it was on to the next base station. With the five modules in place, testing was done to ensure connectivity was maintained, utilizing a well-known routing protocol that could converge incredibly fast if primary links were lost.

At long last, the antennas were planted and the first

ones were laid down. These were the low-frequency radio arrays: copper antennas that were embedded into sheets of Kapton polyimide film. They were remotely placed between the paved roads to each base station – every section was a meter wide and over five kilometers in length. Once connected to the instrumentation modules, these constituted a massive array of tens of thousands of antennas over several hundred square kilometers. This would handle the 30 to 300 kilohertz ranges of the radio observatory.

On the grounds of each base station were receivers to handle various frequencies of the radio spectrum. There were ELF (Extremely Low Frequency) receivers to handle the 3 to 30 hertz range. Each station also had a VLF (Very Low Frequency) receiving antenna installed for the 3 to 30 kilohertz spans. Other frequencies were monitored with a diversity of antennas as well: random wire for high frequency (3 to 30 MHz) and a combined UHF (Ultra High Frequency) at 300 megahertz to 4 gigahertz, VHF (Very High Frequency (30 to 300 MHz)), and multi-band antenna, to name a few.

All of these antennas produced enormous amounts of data once everything began in earnest. Initially, there was a backlog of sending the raw information to the earth via several hops with multiple satellites. This changed in late 2035 with the establishment of the Lunar Fiber Optic Network (LFON), and the floodgates were opened.

Unfortunately, even this proved to not be enough as the data produced rapidly filled the allocated channels. After several more channels were added and their bandwidth was quickly consumed, it was decided to utilize DNA-based storage at Base Esther itself. After a week, the data would be compressed and then sent on through the LFON. The transmitters at Base Netanyahu would have the data sent via laser to an orbiting satellite which would relay it onto other satellites and eventually to the earth.

So it was that even from the frontiers of outer space, at a location on the dark side of the moon, little Israel blessed the nations of the earth even more with scientific knowledge – freely and unconditionally handed over!

Other than the excitement of new knowledge and the occasional visitors, Base Esther was, for the most part, an uneventful duty station.

It was late morning of the 5th of Adar, 5805, which in the Gregorian Calendar also meant Wednesday, the 22 of February, 2045. The Commander of Base Esther was relaxing in his stateroom on a hammock strung between the bunk bed and a hook embedded in the opposite bulkhead. He was wearing the customary light blue jumpsuit with tennis shoes, but he had a towel around his neck as he had just finished the prescribed exercise regime with a quick shower afterwards.

His name was Aitan Rozental and he was a wiry man of 38 years with deep blue-gray eyes. His black hair was already showing some white from all the years of command – which had started shortly after recruit training. A natural computer hacker, he'd found his calling with the C4I Corps, Teleprocessing Corps, of the IDF.

He held the rank of Rav-Seren—a Major—and it was the result of having accepted the post. Normally single, he did have a girlfriend – on the opposite side of the moon at Base Netanyahu. Still, he was fond of telling her that it was better than being a quarter of a million miles away. Geek humor for sure, but there was an aura of truth to it. They did have email and the occasional video chat with none of the delays associated with moon-to-earth communication.

As he slowly swung on his hammock, Aitan Rozenthal held a tablet in one hand and balanced a bowl of his family's hummus in the other. They made Tel Aviv's finest hummus with bragging rights that it was best in Israel. It was also a frequent target of swiping by the twins of his communications center. It was a rare prize, as each member of an upcoming crew was allotted only so much for "perishable personal items" during their trip to the base.

He had a good crew though, and keeping with Israeli

tradition, everyone was on an informal basis. It was split nearly fifty-fifty: civilian and military. Though, with the exception of the current liaison from the Southern Republic, even the civilians were veterans of the IDF.

Savoring the hummus amidst glances at the tablet, he spied a piece of homemade beef jerky on his table – compliments of a crew from the Republic of Texas that had recently visited. In fact, with the garden being a major oasis in the middle of a hostile universe, a system of bartering had developed; Base Esther benefited greatly. The crews from the Southern Republic's Space Exploration Corps always made sure to include kosher vacuum-sealed food for trade and that often included lamb for barbecuing.

He briefly climbed out of his hammock, grabbed the jerky, and sat right back down. His tablet contained documents about the upcoming station audits where drills and exercises would be performed. It broke up the monotony of normal station keeping, though his chief botanist had informed him that she needed help and sadly none could be provided.

Aitan Rozenthal had become so engrossed in reading that he hadn't noticed the arrival of a rather tall, muscular man with green eyes and short brown hair at the open entrance to his stateroom. The Commander's stateroom was designed to look out over the passageway and traditionally had an open-door policy. A loud knock startled him and he nearly dropped his hummus, which elicited a loud guffaw from the man.

"Hello, Brian!" Aitan greeted. "And how is our muscle-bound hero from the Southern Republic doing? Are you here to brag again about your latest weight training goal?" While he set the example by extending his exercise regime an additional quarter of an hour, Brian would always put in an additional hour on the weight resistance for a three-hour total workout. And it showed.

Brian, last name Ascot, was a member of Base Esther's System's Engineering Division. Like Aitan, he too was 38 years of age, but he was built more like an American footballer with his 5'11" frame. His liaison status was a continued symbol of the warm friendship that the State of Israel had with the Republic of Southern States (a.k.a. the Southern Republic).

"No, not this time, boss!" Brian joked back. "But you may want to hide that hummus. We need you in the CIC."

"Really? You couldn't use the intercom?"

"We've detected a signal on the VLF – all of the base stations picked it up."

"Weren't you just running diagnostics?"

"The signal appeared about an hour later. It last nearly two minutes and once it was over, I walked right over to you."

Aitan noticed how serious Brian had become. "VLF, eh?"

"Yes, and it sounded like this." Brian proceeded to whistle a descending tone.

All at once, Aitan's became no-nonsense. "Are you sure?" He quickly cut off Brian's second attempt. "Brian, that's a 'whistler'!" He bolted out of his hammock.

"Yes, I know. I whistled it."

"No, I mean you just *imitated* a 'whistler' and those aren't supposed to be out here. They're produced by lightning and don't extend past some 32,000 kilometers from the earth."

"We were able to compute a general location of about 290 kilometers straight above us." Brian explained matter-of-factly.

"Lead the way!" Aitan briskly followed his friend, hummus and all.

Communications Information Center

Exemplifying its status as the brains of the station, the CIC presented the appearance of a mission control room for spaceflight. In the very center of the main room stood a larger than average console with equally large displays. These were for the communications technicians, designated COMMS 1 and 2. About two meters behind them, in a semi-circular layout, were the consoles for the

System's Engineering Division, the Chief Scientist, a shared one for the cooks, and then separate consoles for the rest: the medics and the Gardener.

Overseeing all of this was the Commander's Station, which consisted of a multitude of displays and workstations. It had a left, right, and front console and occupied nine square meters of space.

Rounding off the main components of the CIC were mounted displays of such a size that everyone could watch what was shared among any console; there were numerous speakers placed in strategic locations as well as smart boards to allow for note-taking and brainstorming sessions.

Numerous open windows and applications on the mounted displays greeted Aitan once he entered the CIC and it took a few moments for him to digest all of the raw data. Once he had, he scanned the room to take stock of just who was with him.

"By the numbers, everyone," he announced. "Abra..."

Abra Ozeri, a woman of 40 with long reddish hair, green eyes, and a marathon-runner's build. She was the Division Head of the Systems Engineers. Still a member of the IDF, she held the rank of Rav nagad—a Chief Warrant Officer—and was also from the C4I Corps.

"At 0800 hours, Brian and Abner commenced array-wide diagnostics," Abra informed Aitan. "They completed their assigned tasks at 0935 with no discrepancies reported. At 1035, all five of the Base Station's VLF receivers detected a signal that lasted 115 seconds. There was no build up to it nor to its cessation. It appeared, lasted for the duration, and then disappeared."

Aitan rubbed his face and nodded. "Abner, do you concur?"

Abner Joachim, aged 32, was a civilian like Brian. He had served his time in the IDF with the infantry and had seen combat. Once his enlistment was over, he joined his family's IT company and earned his degrees through online colleges, honing honed his skills with the toughest certifications – including passing Cisco's hardest-known exam on the first try. He had crew-cut black hair, deep green eyes and at 5'2", he was the shortest member of the current Base Esther crew. However, he was solidly built and often worked out with Brian.

"I concur, Aitan," Abner affirmed. "The array and supporting network are functioning as expected."

Aitan finally glanced at the two men sitting at the Center Console. "COMMS 1 and 2, share your displays with me and then everyone gather around my station.

Ashu and Asher Dahan were identical twins. The youngest of a large family, they tended to act like playful otters – especially when trying to swipe Aitan's hummus. Lanky and socially awkward, they were nonetheless outstanding communications technicians. Their obsession with all things telecommunications began when they were toddlers – helped in large part by their parents, who were both electronics engineers. Their eyes were hazel and their current hair color was brown. Fans of Japanese anime, they tended to favor different hues according to their favorite characters at the time.

They were also a shining example of the *Gedolim b'Madim* – which in English meant Special in Uniform project. Begun in 2008 by a retired IDF Lieutenant Colonel Ariel Almog, the program enabled young men and women with various disabilities to serve in the IDF. In the ordered world of military service and technology, their autism was a benefit; at the age of 27, they both held the rank of Rav samal (Sergeant First Class).

Everyone was silent as Aitan manipulated the open windows, closing some and generally reducing the clutter on the mounted displays. For his own benefit, he played the signal in its entirety and as he listened, he noticed his bowl of hummus was tapped several times. However, every time he glanced at the twins, they just simply smiled and opened their mouths, indication nothing had been swiped. He in turn, just shook his head with bemused disbelief.

"Okay," he addressed them once the playback had ended. "First, this is something that shouldn't be out here." Aitan paused and waited for them to nod in understanding before continuing. "It's called a whistling atmospheric and –"

"It's also called a whistler!" declared an animated Ashu. "An electromagnetic wave propagating through the atmosphere that occasionally is detected by a sensitive audio amplifier as a gliding high to low frequency sound."

"You get that from the online *Britannica*?" Aitan asked.

"Yes! And these electromagnetic waves originate during lightning discharges and are usually in the frequency range of 3000 to 30,000 hertz. That's why the base stations picked it up on the VLF receivers," Ashu added with great excitement.

"And do you need to add anything?" An amused Aitan requested of Ashu's twin brother, Asher. "Maybe I wasn't needed here after all?"

"Yes I do!" Asher answered. "Another source says that their paths reach into the outer space as far as three to four times the earth's radius in the plane of equator and bring energy from lightning discharge to the earth at a point in the opposite hemisphere which is the magnetic conjugate of the position of radio emission for whistlers. From there, the whistler waves are reflected back to the hemisphere from which they started."

"Sounds like *Wikipedia*, Asher!" quipped Aitan.

"And the earth's radius is about 6,371 kilometers, so that means whistlers can be no more than 25,484 kilometers from the earth," Asher imparted.

"I stand corrected, Brian – 25,484 kilometers instead of 32,000!" Aitan admitted with a wide smile, which brought about some chuckling from the Systems Engineers. "But all of these facts fail to explain why this base, located on the dark side of the moon, over a quarter of a million miles from the earth, received a whistler for not just a few seconds but nearly two minutes," Aitan thought out loud. "And I know you all must be thinking about the upcoming station audits."

"That's why we needed you here!" Ashu announced and handed Aitan a tablet. "The *Golda Meir* reported its position to us just before the diagnostics were begun and

Asher and I composed this message for you to approve and send."

Aitan quietly read the contents while Ashu explained more. "We've hidden the actual message with encryption and then disguised that inside a picture. Asher created a one-time-pad as the key for the steganography program."

Raising an eyebrow, Aitan was impressed with the work of the twins. "I approve of this email and the method you two have utilized to hide the message. I'm only adding one line in the email to let the commanding officer of the *Golda Meir* understand that this..." he looked at everyone with a humorless expression, "this is no drill."

The surprised gasps amplified the mood.

"Now, go ahead and send. But first, you guys deserve this." Aitan reached into a drawer at his station and produced two paper bowls. With a plastic spoon, he shared his hummus. Overjoyed, the brothers nearly skipped back to the Center Console.

Aitan and the others observed the twins for a few moments before he spoke up again. He motioned for them to come. "Abra, until the *Golda Meir* can help us figure this all out, I need you and your team to set and enforce CommCon 1, on the firewall. Inspect everything outbound that gets routed onto the LFON." Nodding, they went back to their stations to carry out his order.

Leaning back in his chair, he studied the mounted display that had displayed the signal and the graphic image showed its approximate location. Shaking his head and sighing while rubbing his beard, Aitan slowly, deliberately ate his hummus.

The *Golda Meir*, ISASRV-1898
Location: In Lunar Orbit, 3200 kilometers above Tsiolkovsky Crater

Named after the famed Israeli politician and the first ever woman Prime Minister, the ISASRV *Golda Meir* was a member of the "Pioneering Class" of Space Research Vessels (SRVs). An excellent example of international cooperation, efficiency of design, and superb joint public/

private engineering, SRVs were over 122 meters in length with lunar titanium for their hulls. Despite their size, they only needed a crew of nine to man them.

They weighed in at 1,000 tons with an equal amount of weight in propellant – which was water. Combined with their fusion reactor, they could make between four to six trips to the moon before needing to refill. Normal cruise length was up to 30 days, but with replenishment and the advanced booster, they could make a round trip to Mars in ninety days – 30 days transit, 30 days conducting orbital research, and then 30 days to return.

In appearance, the SRVs could be described as a huge hybrid, ultramodern seaplane with a tri-hull for takeoff speed in the water. Finally, five massive engines could produce anywhere between five and six million pounds of thrust each for a grand total of 30 million pounds. Most of the SRVs also carried a Recon Craft, designated as the Bravo, in a bay on the top of each vessel. The craft could make terrestrial as well as space voyages; the early designs had room for a pilot and a co-pilot or passenger.

Each space-faring nation determined how their own SRVs were named. For example, the Southern Republic Space Exploration Corps (SRSEC) chose the names of women: *Haley*, *Earhart*, *Sally Ride*, *J.G. Low*, and the *Alveda King*. Conversely, the United Kingdom named one of their SRVs the *Churchill*. Crews could be mixed, or strictly an all-male or all-female outfit. Lastly, there was an unofficial tradition that transcended countries and that was how each SRV received their hull numbers: the birth year of their namesakes. Thus, the ISA's *Golda Meir* was designated ISASRV-1898 for Golda Meir's birth year.

She was commissioned in early 2028, and by this time she was on her fourth crew. Crew rotations were based on a four-year tour of duty, followed by a year earth side for refurbishment and mentoring of the next crew. Each refurbishment also included the next "block" of electronics and systems upgrades. With extended mentoring, the all-important aspect of any endeavor was passed on: human knowledge and experience; vital tools for humanity's continued exploration of space.

There was also something special and unique about the current crew, which in 2045 were in the middle of their tour: they were also the original crew of the *Golda Meir* – from the Commanding Officer down to the entire Engineering Department. As Crew Four, they received the customary year-long mentoring from Crew Three. However, the first time around they'd had the opportunity to train with and be mentored by a crew from the Southern Republic.

In the course of nearly five months, they had all become close friends, and the lessons they learned were still being passed on when they returned to the *Golda Meir*. They had been preparing for their latest mission in May of 2030 when the news arrived and it struck them to their very souls: the Southern Republic Exploratory Space Ship (SRESS) *Haley* SRV-1972 had disappeared! Even with the miraculous recovery of the Haley in 2040, where she had been found in orbit around Ceres, there was no closure.

The Bravo was missing and so was her entire crew: Lieutenant David Benjamin, Lieutenant (junior grade) Jason Martinez, Physicians Assistant Johan Slabtonsky, Chief Warrant Officer Jonathan Kohen, Chief Warrant Officer Allen Johnson, Reactor Technician Chiefs Emilio and Hector Gomez, Senior Chief Navigator Matthew Orion, and Environmental Chief Jay Menvy. The whole incident was a mystery; in the SRSEC Manned Spaceflight Incident Report Message, it had been recommended that the crew be labeled KIA: killed in action.

Three women occupied the cockpit of the *Golda Meir* as the vessel maintained its orbital whereabouts. Theirs was a closeness borne of shared sacrifice in the performance of space duty and that included being part of the joint ISA/SRSEC team that flew to Ceres to recover the *Haley*. In fact, once the all-clear had been given, the three had been the first to explore the derelict ship. The return trip had been the longest, most depressing voyage of their lives; when they were given the chance to return to the *Golda Meir* as part of Crew Four, they needed no persuasion.

Floating just over the pilot's seat as she stretched out her 180 centimeter frame was the Commanding Officer, Abana Yaholom. She was the tallest of her crew, and at age 50, the oldest. Her long, wavy brunette hair showed no signs of greying any time soon and her green eyes always seemed to glow in child-like fascination as she explored the cosmos. Her current rank was Sgan-Aluf (a Lieutenant Colonel), and she was a graduate of the Israeli Air Force Flight Academy. A voracious reader, she was also a published author and her current project was a biography of Roni Zuckerman, the first female jet fighter pilot of the Israeli Air Force. For fun, she was a long-distance bicyclist.

Taking advantage of the zero-gravity and sitting cross-legged above the co-pilot's seat was the Chief Engineer of the *Golda Meir*: Seren (Captain) Amalie Meir, aged 46. A navy brat of navy brats, her parents and her parents' parents on both sides had protected Israel through a lifetime of sea duty. So, it was only natural that she too would follow the sweet siren call of the sea.

Amalie was a natural at living up to demanding expectations and family traditions. After nearly three years, she graduated from the Israeli Navy Academy as the outstanding cadet of her class and with a B.A. of mathematics in her hands. That degree in turn led to Master's degrees and eventually to a Doctorate of Engineering as well as a Doctorate of Philosophy – practical married to theory. It suited her well as the Chief Engineer of Crew One. Now 17 years later, she had another PhD in physics, and was nearly completed with her fourth in astrophysics.

As was customary with the rest of the crew, she kept her platinum blonde hair straight and long. Her eyes were a cool gray, reflective of her ability to stay collected in any emergency. Like the rest, she too had an athletic build and at 174 centimeters, she was the third tallest. For fun, she dearly enjoyed her motorcycle and was not one to shy away from getting her hands dirty lugging tools around.

At 173 centimeters, the third woman who floated near Abana was the fourth tallest and her build was that of an endurance swimmer – which was what she did back in Israel for exercise. Her jet-black hair reached all the way to the middle of her back and her light brown eyes matched the color of her skin. She was the Networks Officer, Rav nagad (Chief Warrant Officer) Arial Cohen.

Her parents were Baghdadi Jews who had migrated to Israel from Mumbai, India. Shy by nature, Arial could be quite playful and mischievous once she had become comfortable with someone. A member of the C4I Corps, she had a normal degree in IT, but it was her accomplishments after college that set her apart. She held not one or even two of Cisco's toughest certifications, but *four*, which made her one of the rarest individuals in the entire world. That, and the fact that her resume included a paragraph of additional training and numerous certificates, made her very valuable indeed.

To keep her skills sharp, she possessed an IT lab worth at least a million shekels. In fact, when she wasn't endurance swimming back in Israel, she was always bugging her good friend Amalie about the most efficient way to cool her numerous racks of equipment.

A single woman for much of her life, she had been romantically involved with the first Executive Officer (XO) of the *Haley* – one Kyle DeLeon, who had been transferred just prior to the fateful mission of May 10, 2030. They had reconnected during a joint briefing detailing what little was known of the *Haley's* sudden disappearance and had hit it off. Sadly, Kyle had passed away during her trip to Ceres. His resting place was right next to the monument that South Carolina had constructed in honor of his lost shipmates.

Killing time, the three discussed whatever had been on their minds until Arial's watch glowed, alerting her to a received message. As she quickly floated away to her own station, the XO of the *Golda Meir* returned to the cockpit.

Abira Chagrin, aged 47, could have taken command of another ISASRV but for this crew rotation, she gladly volunteered to be the XO. Her rank was Rav-Seren (Major), and she too was a graduate of the Israeli Air Force Flight Academy. She was the second tallest of the crew at 175 centimeters and sported long, red wavy hair that complimented her hazel eyes.

She was born in the Serbian capital of Belgrade and her parents made Aliyah migrate to Israel when she was five years old. A scrappy fighter from being bullied when she was young, she maintained her phenomenal physique from a lifetime devotion to Krav Maga and held the rank of Expert 5.

Abana, Abira, and Amalie continued their carefree discussions until Arial returned with a tablet. Abana grabbed the device from her and after reading it herself, passed it on to Abira. In moments, the CO and her XO looked at each other with the understanding that came from years of shared service, and while Amalie was reading the message Abana didn't even pipe an announcement to the rest of the crew. No, she used something far more effective as she removed the plastic shield from a red button and pressed it.

The Bravo

With the alarms blaring and the hull of the Bravo creaking, Jonathan and Ozma could only watch the otherworldly light show as they transited the wormhole. Neither said a word as they held hands for support. Lights representing stars flashed by with bewildering speed. It was as if they were traveling through a tunnel of ever-bending light. Then, when it seemed that it wouldn't end, they exited. Jonathan knew from his own experience and training where they were.

He was met with numerous systems failure messages. The Main Engine was offline and nearly all electronics had been automatically shut down. There was limited radio communications remaining; the cockpit display was disabled to conserve power and only the most essential cockpit instruments and screens were engaged. The orbital maneuvering thrusters were still available, but they couldn't be used for any long voyage. Most importantly, the fuel cells ceased functioning and the

Bravo was running on its limited batteries – life support was down to five hours.

Sighing deeply, Jonathan finally informed Ozma, "We're in Earthspace and we're in some sort of orbit on the dark side of the moon. But that's the least of our worries. We're going to need help or in five hours we'll be a floating mystery in space."

Ozma's eyes grew wide as she understood.

Jonathan did his best to hug her despite being constrained in his seat. Their helmets banged against each other, but he calmly whispered, "I'm concerned too."

Comforted by his words, she gripped his hands and waited.

Two hours later
The *Golda Meir*

Five women floated near the table display of the *Golda Meir* as they waited for Abana to finish relaying last-minute orders for Abira in the cockpit and Amalie finished her status checks of the fusion reactor. With her own station near the table display, Arial completed uploading all known data. Everyone wore their full spacesuits as part of being at action stations.

The table display was located at very center of the ship. Physically, it was one meter wide by three meters long. It had touch-screen features and being the Block Four design, it had eight generations of increased capability over the first models. This also included an embedded holographic terminal and a 3-D display of the moon was shown with a question mark indicating an unknown object had been found. A small, vector-like image portrayed the *Golda Meir's* approximate location.

Every crew had their own choice of wallpapers for the table display and this current one was no different: a collage of images of their mentoring days by the crew of the S.R.E.S.S. *Haley*. In the middle of the primary desktop wallpaper was the following: יחכרו לברכה. Translated, it meant, *"May their memory be a blessing"*. Right above Arial's station was an encased signed volleyball – a gift for the *Golda Meir* ladies for their victory over the *Haley* men in the water version of the sport.

Life-long friends Davette Avram and Mahri Allon waited for their boss Amalie to arrive so they could return to their stations in the reactor room. Both were 45 years of age, both held the rank of *Rav nagad* (Chief Warrant Officer), and at 170 centimeters in height, Davette was only one centimeter taller than her dearest friend.

At times they acted more like twins – such as coloring their hair the same hue. Already their green eyes nearly matched and during Crew Four, their long wavy tresses were kept red. Their camaraderie sometimes bordered on an old-fashioned romantic friendship. They trained together, competed in extreme sports together, served in the same unit in the IDF, attended the same college, and were utterly inseparable.

Across from them floated two *Segens* (First Lieutenants). Blith Netanyahu was the Navigator; she and her husband were the proud parents of triplet daughters. With much help from family, a lot of hard work, and an equal amount of emails and voicemails, Blith and her husband Yoni had beaten the odds that long separations in the conquest of space entailed. In fact, their daughters were born exactly nine months to the day Blith had ended her first tour of duty with the *Golda Meir*. At age 43, she was close to earning her PhD in astronomy – a long cherished dream. Back in Israel, she and her family enjoyed long hikes and bike rides for exercise.

She had a cheerful outlook on life and was more than willing to spread that positivity during long voyages. Her musical talents were often requested on routine flight time. With her wide smiles, dimples, sparkling amber eyes, and contagious *joie de vivre* (joy of life), she was the official mascot for crew morale. Unlike the rest of her crewmates, she kept her long brown hair in a bun.

To Blith's side was a woman of equal height—171 centimeters—but with a totally opposite personality:

Danni Almog, the Environmental Officer. Aged 44, quiet, and often with a concerned expression that complimented her blue-gray eyes, Danni's job was often thankless. She had to ensure that the heating, cooling, air conditioning, plumbing, zero-gravity toilets, oxygen levels, carbon dioxide levels, and anything else that might affect the crew's health was kept running. In the process of doing so, she often worked with the ship's physician.

Danni loved having her long, light brown hair floating free during flight, but sadly, the hazards of her job prevented that. There were just too many cramped, dangerous spaces she had to inspect and the only way she could leave her hair untamed would be to cut it. A loner back home, she loved electronic music, online gaming, and was a devout practitioner of yoga.

Floating at one end of the table was a woman who epitomized the power of the human spirit to overcome the odds. She was Seren (Captain) Aizza Dayan, the *Golda Meir*'s physician and a member of Beta Israel – an Ethiopian Jewess.

Her parents were brought to Israel during Operation Solomon: a covert airlift in which the Israeli military brought over 14,000 Ethiopian Jews to Israel in 36 hours. Held between May 24 and May 25, 1991, it had set a world record in which a single El Al 747 carried 1,122 passengers. Upon arrival to Israel, the rescuees were met by ambulances and over 100 received medical care on the tarmac itself.

Like other groups that had undergone Aliyah to Israel, there were major challenges for her parents to overcome and initially it was communications issues, their background of impoverishment, being ill-prepared to work in a developed, industrialized country such as Israel, and finally the worst of all: discrimination and racism.

The latter was still egregious during Aizza's childhood and as a result, she looked to food for comfort. In The Land of Milk and Honey, she had gained excessive weight which only furthered the bullying she received as a child.

While bright and inquisitive, she nonetheless felt the sting of cruel words and being shunned.

But then there was one day in which she had a chance meeting with two incredible people: the 2013 Miss Israel winner Yityish "Titi" Aynaw and Dr. Avraham Yitzhak, who was the first IDF doctor of Ethiopian descent *and* to hold the rank of colonel. Colonel Avraham had also been the first Ethiopian Israeli to serve as a combat doctor in the Paratrooper Brigade and in the elite Maglan Unit.

The meeting influenced Aizza greatly! Here were two fellow Ethiopian Jews that had achieved so much and hadn't let their background stop them. Something in her heart blossomed into a full-blown optimism that she could be so much more, and so she began to walk - slowly and painfully, one kilometer as a start. That single kilometer was met by another and then another. After she had achieved six straight kilometers, she began to run one and then two and then three. She also had made friends with several IDF veterans of Ethiopian heritage and they mentored her. By the time her service in the IDF came up, she had shed a great deal of weight and recruit training removed any excess.

After her initial tour of service, she participated in the "Maayan Program" at Nishmat. The year-long, highly acclaimed program combined Jewish studies with complete support and tools for her personal and professional development and after its completion, she was ready for more. Encouraged by Colonel Avraham himself, she too embarked upon her medical studies and became a doctor and nutritionist.

The ISA sought her out personally and by 2045, she had already authored several vital papers on nutrition in outer space, micro gravity, and low gravity environments such as the moon. Her frame of 172 centimeters was athletic, and Aizza was a stickler for healthy eating - though she did have a soft spot for kosher gummi bears and worms. During spaceflight, she kept her black hair in a long ponytail. Her brown eyes and soft voice had a soothing effect on her patients and fellow crew members.

This Point in Time

With Amalie's arrival, Davette and Mahri returned to their stations in the reactor room and soon after, Abana finally joined everyone else. She waited until the two reported back and then she spoke through the intra-ship intercom.

"Two hours ago, we received an encrypted message from Base Esther. Their message stated that their VLF stations had picked up a signal known as a whistling atmospheric – a.k.a: a whistler. Such signals do not extend past 25,484 kilometers from the earth. Duration of the signal was nearly two minutes and they were able to ascertain a general location of 290 kilometers straight up from Base Esther. Upon receiving this message, I ordered action stations and instructed our Navigator to compute us a course as we were 3200 kilometers above Tsiolkovsky Crater. At 179 kilometers, Blith's radar picked up an object and we proceeded on course. At 62 kilometers, Abira and I were able to view the unknown through the forward optical sensors. Finally, at 30 kilometers from the unknown, we came to a full stop and informed Base Esther."

Taking a deep breath, she continued. "My plan is as follows. With Blith reading out the distances for us, we will maneuver the *Golda Meir* until we are 10 kilometers from the unknown. Once there, Blith will take high-resolution pictures and utilize our Jane's (Jane's Book of International Spacecraft) database to make a possible determination of just what that object is. *If* we get a positive identification, Arial will initiate the SOS Protocol utilizing FSO (free-space optical communications) with infrared. Everyone understand? Good! Blith, please return to your station and start reading out the distances. Davette and Mahri, make sure we have plenty of power in case we have to leave fast. Abira...now!"

In the silence of space, the *Golda Meir* started to close the distance and only Blith's voice interrupted the stillness. "29 kilometers."

Abana just nodded and grunted a quick acknowledgement as Blith continued.

"28...27...26..."

Closer and closer.

Finally, Blith read off a distance of 10 kilometers. "All stop, Abira," Abana ordered. "Okay Blith, what does Jane's say?" she inquired on behalf of the rest of the crew as well.

"Comparing," replied the Navigator.

The pause was almost too great to bear and Abana looked right at Blith. "Jane's says it's most likely a Bravo!"

"Arial," Abana immediately commanded while pointing at her Networks Officer, "go!"

The Bravo

Ozma had been observing Jonathan out of the corner of her eye. His cool demeanor calmed her more than he could ever know. This whole flight, the Bravo spacecraft, the orbital mapping mission – it was *his* world. There was nothing magical she could provide. There was really nothing *either* of them could do at the moment except wait. And this waiting caused an inward turmoil that Ozma had never felt before.

Oh my dear, dear brother, she thought. *If only Mother could help us now. I wish I could tell you, but I can't. And now we are in your world. For what reason? Why? I'm worried. I look at you and you're so collected. I know you said you were concerned too but why are we here? Time is running out for us. Time... Why after all my years am I now in humanity's world?*

Suddenly, one of the few remaining instrument displays lit up and its illumination caught both Jonathan's and Ozma's attention. "Jonathan..." She barely managed to get her words out and pointed, dragging his hand along with hers. "It's saying SOS PING received from the FSO channel."

A long string of numbers appeared with a smaller one which counted upwards. She read off the long one. "It's saying that it came from two-zero-zero-one colon -d-b-eight colon eight-three-seven-nine colon eight-three-zero-zero colon colon 5." She was excited as her fingers hovered over the display. "What does it mean? Please explain it to me!"

His own eyes had lit up with glowing relief as he examined the display. "Ozma," he said, "it means that somebody out there has reached out to us. You just read off a special address for what's called the 'SOS Protocol' for spacecraft."

"What do those numbers counting up mean?" She pointed.

"The Protocol states for the sending spacecraft to repeat that signal 256 times. It's already at 180."

"Then what happens?"

"Our system will automatically transmit 32 pings back to them. It'll be sent to their 'colon colon one' address. They—whoever they are—must be close for this to happen. If we were unconscious, the system would wait for 30 seconds and then a repeating group of 16 pings would be sent with 30-second intervals between them."

"But we're not!"

"No! And as you can see, we've just sent ours back. The screen is waiting for us to touch the SOS REQUEST for a manual response. Go ahead and touch it, and I'll explain."

Ozma did as he asked and she was greeted with more numbers and an 'SOS STATUS MESSAGE' transmitted. She grabbed his hands in eager anticipation and pointed at what appeared on the display:

2001:db8:8379:8300:1972:1120:8000:1994.

"We've seen the first groups and those constitute the SOS Protocol," he calmly explained. "Now the '1972' means—"

"That was the *Haley's* hull number!"

"Yes! And the last group of numbers mean the property book entry - or in this case, the identification number for the Bravo."

"So, we just sent a message meaning we're from the *Haley's* Bravo!" Ozma's face lit up in wondrous understanding as she gestured to the contents of the message. "'Passengers'. That means us and it says two."

"Yes."

"'Status of Life Support' and it says 'Critical'. Is that bad?"

"Very, and the numbers next to it are telling them we have just under three hours left."

"'Status of Main Engines' and the 'Unusable' must mean we can't use them?"

"Unless we get them fixed or replaced – which isn't happening out here. They're damaged beyond feasibility somehow."

"It's saying our maneuvering thrusters are 'nominal', but I know you just use those to position the Bravo. The 'System Status' has just phrases and numbers?"

"Basically, it's a tiny log dump that the other side can examine through their own database. All of this info is just text that can be sent quickly – their own system will give a graphic readout."

"The 'Date and Time Stamp'; where does that come from?" Ozma inquired.

"That's from the Internal Systems Clock. It starts once the Bravo's manufacturer engages all of the systems for the first time while it's still in the factory. It's a highly accurate clock too – used by the maintenance folks to determine age of the Bravo. It's internal battery will last decades." He placed their hands back on the center console.

"Now we wait, then?" she rightfully observed. "That display also has a little keyboard for us to tell them something?"

She saw his nod and was satisfied.

"Jonathan?" she almost whispered.

"Yes, Ozma?"

"Thank you. Thank you for being so calm..."

He chuckled at her words and squeezed her hand. Even through the gloves, she knew it was a sign of compassion and appreciation.

"That's something they beat into us at the Academy and every moment during flight school. 'Panic kills oxygen' the instructors would say. And since we need oxygen to live..."

"Panic kills in space," Ozma stated, finishing his sentence.

The *Golda Meir*

I cannot believe what I am seeing. This has got to be some kind of exercise, Abana said to herself after the message had been received and everyone had let loose an audible gasp. *There is no way that craft is saying it's November 3rd, 2030.* After a pause of some thirty vital seconds, she finally broke through her daze.

"So you're telling me that we received SOS pings back and a STATUS MESSAGE from the *Haley's* Bravo - a spacecraft that's been missing for nearly 15 years? With two passengers who are most likely alive?" she demanded.

Arial could only nod.

"Okay. Here, type this message: We are the ISASRV *Golda Meir*. Who are you?"

Arial did as she was asked and they were met with a response: *I am Jonathan Kohen, with a passenger. Please help.*

Still shaking her head, Abana typed the next message herself: *Why did you guys humiliate us in water volleyball?*

There was light chuckling as Abana smirked; an impostor wouldn't know how to answer.

The response: *I don't know what you're talking about. You ladies beat us pretty well and you got a signed volleyball!*

Utter pandemonium ensued, gasps of disbelief as everyone tried to speak at once.

"Everyone!" Abana commanded, waiting for quiet. "Calm...calm. By the numbers now. Abira will maneuver us to within 300 meters. Blith, get the USV (unmanned space vehicle) ready with a tether. Good thing our own

Bravo wasn't brought along for this trip. Arial, inform them of what we are doing. Everyone else, we'll point the Golda Meir at the Bravo and enable the video links so you can also watch for anything at your own workstations. Let's rescue them – they've only got hours of life support left. We can ask more questions when they are aboard. Let's go!"

The Bravo

"After all we've been through, it just had to be the *Golda Meir*!" Ozma uttered as the Bravo was being towed. She watched how Jonathan simply leaned back in his pilot's seat and breathed a deep sigh of relief.

"They'll probably have a lot of questions – especially about me," she quipped.

He chuckled at her comment. "No doubt, Ozma. No doubt."

Just then, the Bravo entered the *Golda Meir*'s bay and the strong lights caused both to pull down the sun visors on their helmets. With several gentle thuds, the Bravo was secured and the bay doors closed overhead. Ozma watched as Jonathan pressed a number of buttons and threw several switches.

"Are you shutting down everything?" She asked and he softly answered yes. Finally, the Bravo became silent and dark; she copied his movements, unlatching her belts.

"Please let me follow you."

"Sure thing," he replied, and she handed him their tablets – which he placed into a pocket. With his pilot's side hatch opened, he began to float out with Ozma in tow.

"Zero gravity is fun!" She giggled but she didn't have much time to enjoy it. Ozma noticed him opening a gray hatch and he pulled her along into a tunnel. It wasn't as bright as the bay, but both kept their sun visors down. Looking back, Ozma noticed that the hatch slowly closed by itself and with a whooshing noise, she could feel air hitting her suit.

They both stopped at a second hatch and Ozma held

him tight and whispered, "Let's go and let what will happen, happen."

He opened the hatch.

The *Golda Meir*

Abana hovered near the table display with a stoic look on her face. As she observed the hatch to the upper bay opening, she quickly glanced behind her at Abira with a Tavor. "Regulations," she quipped before returning to keeping tabs on her assembled crew.

In floated one person. "Well, it's a Southern Republic space suit...," she whispered.

A shorter, second person was right behind the first and remained close. There was an awkward pause once the hatch closed automatically and everyone seemed to be sizing each other up.

Finally, the taller person removed their helmet.

"Oh my gosh!" were the only words she managed to get out as the crew gasped in united surprise.

"It's *Yehonatan*!" She heard the rest say, recognizing Jonathan as she removed her own helmet and placed one hand to her mouth, grasping an edge of the table display with the other. She heard Abira's gasp behind her and with a nod, she quietly sent her Second-in-Command back to secure the Tavor away.

He doesn't look a day over 45! How? she pondered and shook her head, waiting for the next person to introduce themselves. Over and over, she could see hands touching his face and suit, as if everyone was trying to prove to themselves what their hearts were denying.

The second person only lifted their visor and a second shock, more than the first, temporarily overwhelmed all who saw her.

Complete and utter disbelief was what Abana observed from her crew; everyone was uncertain and silent. "But the Haley didn't have a female crew member!" she thought out loud and bumped Abira, who had returned. "I know." Abana acknowledged when she overheard Abira repeat the same thing. Quickly, she took a picture with her suit camera.

"Welcome aboard the ISASRV *Golda Meir*," she finally announced, and her voice broke the spell of silence that had affected her crew. Floating towards the new passengers, she stopped in front of Jonathan, placed her hands on his shoulders, and then gave him a strong bear hug. "We were told you were killed in action," she whispered, and several tears of joy became shiny, translucent globes that floated off her cheeks.

She then went to shake the hand of the woman next to Jonathan. "*Shalom*, I am Abana Yahalom, Commanding Officer of this vessel. I am pleased to meet you."

The very first thing Abana noticed was that the woman in front of her had the deepest green eyes she had ever seen. "I am Ozma, Ozma Tippetarius, and I want to thank you for rescuing us." Her voice was soft and soothing.

"Ozma," Abana replied, "I am honored. But I must say on behalf of my crew that we are still confused by your presence with our dear friend Yehonatan. His ship—the *Haley*—didn't have any..." Abana tried to state as politely as possible.

Ozma gently took her hands. "I more than understand. If it helps, I was once a boy," she declared with a wide grin.

Abana and the rest didn't know what to make of Ozma's revelation and the crew became silent once again. It was an awkward moment, and Abana noticed that Ozma was blushing. "You are a friend of *Yehonatan's*, you are a friend of ours," she affirmed with a hand on Ozma's shoulder.

"Now," Abana announced, "we will be taking our guests and their Bravo to the Adjunct Base next to Base Esther. I am more than certain we all have many questions and those will be answered, in time. I am asking that *Yehonatan* and Ozma follow Amalie down to the Engineering section – we have spare seats for them. Everyone, take up landing stations!"

Before Jonathan could leave, Abana grabbed his arm and pulled him aside. "Do you know what year this is?"

"We crash-landed around May 13th? We've been there less than six months – it's November 3rd, 2030."

Abana looked right into his eyes and gulped. *"Yehonatan,* it's the 5th of Adar, 5805." She saw him trying to convert the date so she did it for him. "Today is February 22, 20...45"

His eyes became wide as he stared at her, agape.

She had to leave him speechless as Mahri floated up to them and led him away. Out of the corner of her eye, she noticed Amalie and Ozma were talking and she paused her journey up to the cockpit to find out why.

"Mind explaining?" She inquired once her Chief Engineer arrived.

"Oz—Miss Tippetarius—told me something."

"Yes, her name is Ozma. What did she say?"

"Ozma said *Yehonatan* had mentioned an Einstein-Rosen Bridge – a wormhole."

Base Esther
Communications Information Center

What is going on? Aitan thought as he leaned back in his seat. The CIC was eerily quiet and empty. Once he had read the message from the *Golda Meir's* Commanding Officer, he had ordered everyone to the mess (dining room). His self-imposed isolation wasn't helping him understand the recent events, and he gazed up at the mounted displays and then back down to a tablet he held.

One display had a full-screen picture titled "S.R.E.S.S. *Haley* SRV-1972, Crew Picture 05 MAY 2030." The other had retrieved news articles about the crew as well as a picture of one of the crew members: Chief Warrant Officer Three Jonathan Kohen.

There was also another picture that he kept maximizing and then minimizing. He wanted to share this one with Brian once he arrived. His eyes returned to the tablet and he read over the highlighted last section. It was part of an archived email that dated back to Tuesday, July 24th, 2040.

"Line 9 (FINAL COMMENTS): User jkohen initiated the ping6 -s 1964 2001:db8:1972::2 command. Recommend crew be labeled KIA. Unknown as to why HALEY disappeared. Unknown as to why HALEY was found in orbit around Ceres. Suggest long-term review of all existing video, audio, and system logs to ascertain potential cause. Inform any remaining next of kin.

Very respectfully,

CDR Jon Williams Kryton

SRSEC Spacecraft Recovery Branch

SYAEAE"

Out of the corner of his eye, he noticed Brian's entrance. "What's the news?"

"Everyone except Chatulah."

Aitan chuckled in response. "I'm not surprised. She demands that everyone call her by her nickname and then she tries to live the life of a cat here, doing her own thing. She's still a member of the crew and I'm still her boss. When you're done here, go grab her, will ya?"

"Sure thing, boss. What's up?"

"Here, read the email first." Aitan handed him the tablet. He carefully watched for Brian's reaction. "Is this the first time you've read it?

"No, but it's been a couple of years, I think."

"Okay, now look up at the mounted displays, but I need you to be sitting next to me – here's a chair. It's going to get deep really, really fast."

"Okay, the first one is the *Haley* crew before they took off on May 10th, 2030. I saw her take off that day. A bunch of us held a banner for them on the Arthur Ravenal Jr. Bridge," Brian recalled.

"That must have been something to watch," Aitan commented. "I've been to Charleston a couple of times myself – always during the summer. I'm a glutton for punishment I guess." Both men snickered.

"We're not here discussing Charleston, are we?"

"No. The next display has some news articles about

the *Haley's* disappearance and the eventual discovery. There's also a picture—"

"That one is Chief Kohen, the *Haley's* Network Officer."

"Correct. The email recommended that the entire crew be labeled Killed In Action."

"That's right; the crew was missing when the *Haley* was discovered," Brian added.

"Yes, and a large amount of the ship's removable gear was found to be missing – including all personal items *and* the Bravo."

"Yeah, that was odd since that version could only handle two passengers, not an entire SRV crew."

Aitan waited a few moments. "The *Golda Meir* just recovered that Bravo."

Brain nearly dropped the tablet. "Really? So that was the source of the 'whistler' we received?"

"No, the radio wasn't broadcasting."

"I don't understand."

"Welcome to the club."

Aitan began to explain the events. "They first detected the Bravo using their radar – at a distance of 179 kilometers. At 62 kilometers, the CO and XO were able to get a visual using the forward optical sensors."

"That's because the SRVs utilize an array of high-definition cameras for the cockpit."

"Yes, in keeping with the required aerodynamics. The SRVs have only one physical window and it's on the outer door," Aitan told Brian. "So, they got the *Golda Meir* to a distance of 30 kilometers and then they came to a full stop and informed us here." He waited until Brian nodded in acknowledgement. "Finally, they got to a distance of 10 kilometers, retrieved a very detailed picture, and then ran Jane's against it."

"When it was determined to be a Bravo, did they go up and retrieve it?" Brian asked.

"No, they first initiated the SOS Protocol. It was the

CO's call."

"If anything, they would have gotten back the automated response, and then a group of 16 pings every 30 seconds."

Aitan looked right at Brian and slowly, yet firmly delivered the unbelievable news: "Brian, the *Golda Meir* received an SOS REQUEST and soon after an SOS STATUS MESSAGE."

Brian's response was utter disbelief. "That's not possible. The Bravo's life support would never last past a week!"

Aitan didn't reply, glancing straight ahead at the mounted display with a picture of Chief Kohen. "I told you it was going to get deep really fast," he said after a while. "The Internal Systems Clock gave a date of November 3rd, 2030." He looked at Brian while he tapped the tablet and the picture he had minimized sprang up next to the one of Kohen.

"There were two passengers on that Bravo. This picture was taken just after they were aboard."

Aitan could only watch as Brian became faint and sank into his chair.

"That's no photo-manipulation, and yes, you are also seeing a *female* next to Chief Kohen," Aitan continued. "And yes, we both know the *Haley* had no female crew members."

Brian's shocked silence was what Aitan had anticipated and he allowed his mate several minutes to collect his thoughts before speaking again. "The *Golda Meir* will be landing soon at the Adjunct Base. It's a good thing that place is basically remotely managed. I'll be taking the train once I'm done talking with you. The facilities there will keep the *Golda Meir's* crew occupied while this whole incident is figured out. I'm also asking if you wouldn't mind having a roommate during this time."

"You mean the girl?" joked Brian, but he received a swift smack on the shoulder.

"You Southern Republic boys are supposed to be

gentlemen," Aitan declared with his best imitated southern accent.

"Just kidding, boss!" Brian retorted. "I've just never had a ghost for a roomie." Both laughed. "Now, who's the lucky volunteer?"

Aitan smirked and Brian snorted. "I know our dear Chatulah has been stressed lately – strike that; *extremely* stressed."

"We have a saying where I'm from: choose your rate, choose your fate."

"That's cold, Brian!"

"Not as cold as the shadows on the surface," Brian countered.

"True. Very, very true. Deadly too."

"You like living on the edge. I'm glad I'm only grabbing her from the Garden."

"The privileges of being the Commander." Aitan rose from his seat. "I'll also grab some extra clothes from the Adjunct. I'll be going now. This has been quite a day and it's nowhere near over yet…"

Chatulah and Ozma

I'm tired, overwhelmed, smell like garbage, Brian didn't give me a chance to at least hose down, and now I have to play babysitter, Chatulah bitterly thought to herself. She had spilled an 18-liter container of table scraps meant for the composting bin – a newly added feature of the Garden. The old food had had some time to decompose inside the sealed container and mushy food remains had poured over her. She stank, and the rest of the crew reminded her of that as they waited – she sat in one corner of the mess and the others stood far away.

As they walked to the washroom module, she kept on spying on her charge with stolen glances. The young woman walked with a gait that reminded her of British royalty – a little too snobbish for her own liking *I don't care if she's rescued; I am so far behind getting everything done.* Their introduction in the mess had been rather awkward with both having to repeat their names several times. Sighing deeply, she begrudgingly accepted her fate as they entered the washroom.

"You can go first, Ozma," Chatulah informed her. "I really need to wash twice." She gave her a visitor's badge to swipe. Turning away to give Ozma some privacy, she only started to disrobe once Ozma had entered the shower section. Then there was simply quiet.

"Um, Chatulah?"

Oh for the love of... Chatulah nearly said outright and donned a towel before peeking around the entrance. "Ozma?"

"I've..." the woman hesitated. "I've never used a shower before."

"What are you then," Chatulah blurted out in frustration, "a princess who needs someone else draw her a bath?"

She immediately regretted her words.. "My apologies, Here, you take this badge and wave it over this little square. Once you do, you'll get a rinse that lasts for 30 seconds. After you've lathered up with the body wash in this pink bottle, push this green button and you'll get 45 seconds to rinse everything off. I'm...I'm sorry for yelling at you."

Ozma's soft smile and deep green eyes soothed Chatulah's spirit and as Ozma washed, she got herself ready.

Twenty minutes later, both were in Chatulah's stateroom. Again, both women remained quiet and Ozma climbed the ladder to her part of the bunk bed and got under the covers. In moments, she was soundly asleep; Chatulah had been observing her the entire time.

Climbing into her own bed, she commenced reading her *Tanakh*. Unfortunately, her mind was racing and it made study difficult. Minute by minute, as she perused the Psalms, she began to relax and unwind. She yawned at the beginning of Psalm 116 and by verse 19, her eyes were heavy and her body became paralyzed with sleep.

Hours later, she abruptly woke. After ensuring that

Ozma was still asleep, she checked on her great-grandmother's picture. For some time, Chatulah just stood there, looking over the young girl with silent tears streaming down her face.

6ᵀᴴ OF ADAR, 5805
(THURSDAY, 23 FEBRUARY 2045)

It was a desert Ozma had never seen before. The dark gray sand was coarse on her bare feet as she walked, drawn by an unknown need to see the hills in the distance. The air was hot and acrid, as if the heat of thousands of ovens and bonfires radiated from a specific spot in the sky. Above, the sun was partially hidden by smoke.

There was a nearly silent hum in the air as she got closer to the hills. Then Ozma saw what they really were: millions upon millions of piles of shoes, clothes, watches, and jewelry as far as the eye could see. Vast numbers of chests containing pieces of gold embedded into fragments of white material lined the boulevards that separated the mounds.

Without warning, the hum fell away and all around her became silent – so much so that her heart sounded like a bass drum inside her ears. From out of nowhere, a still small voice spoke; all it said was, "Ask for her forgiveness."

She was confused. "Why do I need to? What have I done wrong?" asked. For long moments, all remained as muted as before.

Suddenly, wave after wave of translucent bands of energy flowed all around her. As they wisped every which way, they began shriek. At first, Ozma could tell it was a man or a woman in agony, but then the voices started merging. Soon, it was one vast collection: thousands upon thousands. A great combined voice of young and old men, women, boys, and girls; healthy, sick, disabled, and able-bodied. These were the lives cut short by the evil of one man.

It greatly startled Ozma, which caused her to step back. Immediately, a stabbing pain shot up from her toe and she reached down to see what it was. Something had jabbed her and grasping it, Ozma realized that it was a tiny bone. But from what? her heart pondered. As she held it in her hand, it began to crumble into the same kind of dark gray sand and a breeze blew it up and away.

The shoes, clothes, jewelry – everything had belonged to people. The shrieks were their horrific last moments and the bands of energy represented their souls.

This wasn't sand.

It was human ash...

Ozma awoke when she heard the alarm and she felt the bunk bed stir as Chatulah rose and headed into the water closet. Rubbing her eyes, she glanced at the smart screen that displayed the numbers "0500". "It's earlier than I'm used to," she whispered. The room itself gained more illumination as the door to the water closet leaked soft radiance, which gave Ozma an opportunity to examine her surroundings.

Quickly realizing that the room was a spartan affair, she just waited for Chatulah to emerge. Since the door wasn't thick, she heard a variety of sounds and quietly giggled a couple of times. Finally, the door opened and Chatulah already had donned a light blue jumpsuit and socks. Ozma spoke up once Chatulah had sat in a chair to loosen the straps of her shoes.

"Good morning!" she announced cheerfully, even though Ozma was still becoming more awake herself.

"It is morning," was the response.

"Where are you going?"

"To the mess and then to work."

"Where do you work?"

"You ask a lot of questions for a stranger," Chatulah curtly replied before she stood.

"I'm sorry, I'm just curious." Ozma stated with a bit of shock at the response.

"I am the Chief Botanist here."

"I don't understand." Ozma said, slightly shaking her head.

"I'm the assigned gardener." Chatulah made known with her hands on her hips.

"Oh! There's a garden *here*? Under the moon? Please, may I see it?" Ozma inquired as she sat up in bed.

"I don't have time to be a tour guide. If I don't work long hours each day, much fruit and vegetables will be lost."

Ozma excitedly climbed down from the top bunk and asked, "May I help you?" And she even put a hand to her mouth in shock. *Where did that come from?* she thought, but she repeated, "Please, let me help you."

There was a look of genuine surprise on her roommate's face. "You don't look like you're the working kind." Chatulah answered with raised eyebrows and crossed arms.

"I know, many back where I'm from boast that I haven't worked a day – ever. I...I used to be a slave. The woman who had changed me into a boy treated me so terribly and I had to work late around her farm – cultivating her corn fields, milking the cow, and feeding her pigs." Ozma told as she shared her background.

There was an awkward pause as Ozma observed Chatulah's look of utter disbelief; the words had taken her aback. "You'll find nothing of the sort here," Chatulah finally stated. "Pigs are *treif* – non-kosher."

Ozma was crestfallen and stared at the floor. As she started to climb back up, however, she felt a hand on her shoulder. "I'm sorry, Ozma," Chatulah whispered. "It'll be very long days...I've been so stressed about things and the lack of help has weighed on me heavily."

Ozma took Chatulah's hand and gently squeezed. "I understand. I'm probably the *last* person you'd request for help." She noticed a slight smile creeping onto Chatulah's face.

"It won't take me long to get dressed and ready."

"All right," Chatulah finally acquiesced. "The water closet has an extra pair of gloves. Let me grab them."

In moments, Ozma had put on a similar light blue jumpsuit, her socks, and slipped into her shoes. When Chatulah reemerged, she was more than pleasantly surprised.

"I'm ready!" Ozma proclaimed and the grin she received warmed her heart. She closed the door behind them as Chatulah led the way.

The Mess - 0730

It is often said that superb morale is enabled from first-class chow created by exceptional cooks. For Base Esther, that was embodied by the husband and wife team of Judah and Lenah Shaked. With their combined Jewish heritage, and Judah's Puerto Rican ethnicity and Lenah's Arabic background, their culinary talents were in high demand. Indeed, they were already scheduled to be part of the cooking staff at Base Netanyahu once their current tour was over.

Lenah was the shorter of the two, with brown eyes and shoulder-length brown hair. Her personality was bubbly and her permanent smile was contagious. Though aged 24, she looked like she was 19. Judah, 29, was the more serious one of the pair, but he enjoyed a good laugh and his hearty guffaws could be heard almost on the other side of the base. He kept his dark hair short and had a slight beard and mustache. As followers of the Nazarene, they were also a minority of a minority.

Their domain consisted of three large round tables and several booths with bar stools. Plants were strung everywhere and several foldable displays provided different scenes of home. There was a large display at one end that was used during important base meetings or for movie nights. Overall, it had a cozy feel to it. Their galley was a model of efficiency and compactness – all based on military field kitchen technology.

This morning's scrumptious breakfast was steak- courtesy again of the Republic of Texas – eggs, and par boiled and pan-fried potatoes. The mess had a delightful aroma to it and the air held a mixture of Hebrew and English words.

Aitan stood by one of the booths with a large mug of herbal tea, discussing the previous night's events with his medics as they ate. There was Efren Levy, aged 42, and holding the rank of Rav samal rishon (Master Sergeant). He was a well-built man with salt and pepper hair that he kept short, but not too short like Judah's. He had blue-green eyes with an inquisitive look about them. He loved to read and enjoyed mixed martial arts when back home.

Next to Efren sat the other medic assigned to Base Esther: Samal rishon (Staff Sergeant) Bethesda Kimhi. Aged 26, this was Bethesda's first tour as a medic for the ISA. She had long, strawberry blonde hair that flowed to the middle of her back and she owned several pairs of contacts that tinted her eyes. She loved videogames and often competed against Ashu and Asher during their free time. For exercise, she enjoyed long distance running.

Efren and Bethesda were members of the renowned IDF Emergency Medical Team, IDF Medical Corps' field hospital, and both had been deployed worldwide for every kind of catastrophe. The situations they had faced and the experience gained turned out to be an ideal fit for the ISA's Medical Corps.

Aitan then strolled over to the table where Jonathan, Brian, Abra, and Abner reclined and ate. "Watch your portion size, *Yehonatan.*," he quipped. "Not as many calories needed here on the moon!" Jonathan showed that he only had had only a little more steak. "Great food?" he inquired.

"My compliments to the chefs."

"I thought so! Brian, I see you got your fellow Southern Republic gentleman to wear his sleeves up," Aitan commented and laughed when Brian and Jonathan gave each other a fist bump. "Did you tell him about the 'Fortuitous Five' back in Ohio of the United States?" When Brian said he had forgotten, Aitan filled in for him.

"Get this, *Yehonatan*: five guys from Ohio bet that Cleveland would win both the World Series and the Super Bowl – utterly astronomical odds...they'll never have to work again!" Everyone laughed.

"Brian, can you remember their names?" Aitan quizzed. After a while, Brian answered, "That would be Ferencik, Coyne, Mantle, Macalla, and let me see...yeah, Principi. Greatest return on investment in history."

"Lucky indeed," Aitan then. "Everyone, let's have a toast to our 'ghost'! Lenah, please grab one of those bottles of Texas spring water." She did and also returned with cups for everyone in the mess, filling them before she went on to the next person. With their cups in the air, Aitan was about to say *"L'Chaim"* when Jonathan's hold slipped and he spilled some water on his left forearm.

Aitan chuckled along with everyone else and lightly ribbed Jonathan for his clumsiness. That humor disappeared once he noticed the water move by itself, forming what looked like a patch of clear gel. He saw Jonathan try to shake it off but it had stuck fast. Grabbing a nearby paper towel, he was walking up to hand it to Jonathan when the material turned deep red and scream shattered the peace. Jonathan had collapsed to the floor in terrible pain with his arm smoking!

Everything became a blur as Aitan witnessed his crew's instinctual response. Lenah announced, "Medical emergency in the mess," on a nearby base intercom, and also pressed an emergency button activating flashing lights and video cameras. Her husband tossed the galley's first aid kit to Efren. And out of the corner of his eye, Aitan saw Bethesda take off running to retrieve the medic's kit.

Brian, Abra, and Abner were desperately trying to comfort Jonathan as he writhed on the floor. The material on his arm had changed into a singed red mass and was bubbling. Soon, the sickly smell of burnt flesh permeated the air. Efren leaned over to render aid when *zap!*

Tiny electrical tendrils violently reacted to the presence of Efren's hands and he leaped back in pain. Bethesda arrived just after and her efforts to examine Jonathan's arm received the same cruel treatment.

Aitan could only look on with eyes wide in horror as a sound similar to that of chicken frying in hot, rancid grease came from Jonathan's arm. He could feel his stomach churn as those closest to Jonathan turned green at the sight and stench.

"Lenah," Aitan barely managed to shout as the bile neared the top of his throat, "do you know where..." "His friend was with Chatulah earlier," Lenah quickly answered her boss. said "she was helping."

"Go!" Aitan gasped and Lenah ran.

Time slowed down for Aitan as he waited. That was all he *could* do. With Jonathan in utter agony, it was all Brian, Abra, and Abner could do to restrain him. An oven mitt had been placed into his mouth to allow him to bite down. With the medics prevented from assisting, the waiting was painful for them as well; Aitan saw it in their expressions. He noticed Efren retrieving a tourniquet, which meant he was thinking worst-case scenario. The smell in the room had become unbelievably noxious.

In the nick of time, Lenah returned with Chatulah and Ozma – who were covered in mud. Aitan simply pointed at Jonathan so Ozma could go to him. He saw her eyes grow wide at his condition and she reached for him. The little bolts of lightning seemed to have no effect on her. Aitan glanced at his medics, who were just as mystified.

"Jonathan?" Aitan heard Ozma start to ask, but she was interrupted instead by wild spasms from Jonathan's body and shrieks that were somehow even louder than before. "I take that as a yes..." She acknowledged.

Aitan watched in amazement as Ozma's hands hovered over the material and then a soft green glow emanated from them. This glow came into contact with Jonathan's arm and immediately the sizzling sound ceased. She grasped his arm and it began to glow as well. His screams subsided and his body began to relax. Her hands then lifted the material so all could see it being surrounded by a globe of swirling colors that were various hues of green, red, blue, yellow, and purple.

Aitan's mouth was just agape in wonderment at the scene. "My gosh," was all he could say. The entire mess had become quiet as Ozma continued working. She directed the globe towards a metal tray on a nearby table and laid the object down. Then, as she waved her hands, Aitan saw particles in the air start to collect until they became a golf-sized, dark green ball.

His nostrils knew immediately what Ozma had done and Aitan noticed everyone's responses as well. The disgusting stench had been removed! He looked at Judah, who grabbed an air-tight container and brought it to Ozma. She floated the vile orb into the container and Judah quickly sealed it.

Aitan, Efren, Bethesda, and Ozma then went to Jonathan as Brian, Abner, and Abra released him. Aitan saw that his left forearm was red, like a sunburn, but his face advertised that he was free of the intolerable pain. His eyes had shed quite a few tears and Bethesda wiped them away as well as removed the oven mitt. Slowly, Jonathan sat up.

"We were just about to have a toast when he spilled some water on his arm." Aitan explained and Ozma nodded in understanding. "He'd been drinking tea with his breakfast. It was just some bottled spring water from Texas."

Aitan could sense that Ozma was thinking and the rest of his crew were also nodding in agreement. "Texas," Ozma said. "Aitan, I remember being told about The Republic of Texas from Jonathan and David during our first meeting."

"Yes, Miss Tippetarius," he answered. "They are one and the same. An SRV from that nation recently visited here and the crew traded a good deal of food and drink to spend time in our garden."

"Texas. Is that from the earth?"

"Yes, why?" Aitan was nudged by Jonathan. "You don't have to talk..." he affirmed as Jonathan was given some ice chips.

I can't begin to understand what just happened, Aitan thought. *Good thing for the cameras running; even I don't believe what I just saw go down. It was just water. Water from the—"*

"Earth!" he nearly shouted. "We use purified water from lunar ice. As crazy as it sounds, earth water must be dangerous for him."

He felt faint at the thought of what might have been had Jonathan drank that water. "I am at a loss as to what's going on here," he admitted to everyone but directed his glance towards Ozma and Jonathan. "On behalf of *Yehonatan*, I want to thank you, Miss Tippetarius—"

"Please, just Ozma," she insisted.

"Ozma, thank you for healing him—and our noses really appreciate what you did after—but I am going to require that both of you report to the medical bay for observation. I hope you understand."

"I do, Aitan," Ozma said, nodding in agreement, and Aitan saw Jonathan's weak smile concurring as well.

"Efren and Bethesda, grab your kit and head on over to the medical bay. Abra, have the Twins send an encrypted message to the Commanding Officer of the *Golda Meir* requesting that she and the Physician come over to assist in the examination," Aitan commanded. "Lenah, bring that metal tray to the medics once everyone is out of here."

His crew scattered to carry out their orders and he started walking away but then he paused, rubbed his beard, and spoke up.

"Chatulah, go ahead and get Ozma to the showers first and then bring her over. And when you've done that, go over to my station in the CIC. Until Ozma is released from the medics, *I'm* your help."

Her wide smile was all Aitan needed to see.

Hours later
A Commander's Meeting

Abana shook her head as she waited for Aitan to join her. "All my years of service and all of the combined experiences of my own crews never prepared me for what the past 24 hours have revealed," she said to herself. "I don't know if I'm living in a movie or I've knocked my head and this is all a dream."

She held one tablet and another lay in her lap. The one in her hand contained the results of the medical examinations and the other was from Arial – with incredible findings all of her own regarding the recovered Bravo.

"*Shalom*, Aitan!" she said once he arrived and had sat down opposite of her.

"*Aleichem Shalom*, Abana!" he replied. "Sorry for the delay. I've been busy helping Chatulah until Ozma is okay to return and resume assisting her."

"I can smell that," she quipped. "Chatulah? I remember meeting her at Base Netanyahu. She's...one of a kind. Keeps to herself for the most part – every bit her feline nickname."

"She is!" Aitan laughed. "She's good though; the finest Chief Botanist the ISA has. An amazing history too – her great-grandmother survived Auschwitz, married a fellow Jewish survivor, and fought in the Palmach. Chatulah's confided to me that her great-grandmother's dying wish was to avenge her people, the Romani. She even has a hand-drawn picture from her of the one who sent them to Southern Europe."

"That 'person' is more or less dead by now," Abana countered.

"Unless they're immortal," he retorted and both chuckled heartily for some time.

Then the pair became quite serious.

"This has been the most incredible non-exercise of my life, Aitan," she confessed.

"I know. I still can't believe what I witnessed earlier."

"I saw that video. And what Ozma did. I'm right with you. Speaking of which, shall we start with our totally unknown and mysterious female guest?"

"Yes," Aitan answered. "Ozma did request to pass on her deep gratitude to Doctor Dayan for putting her completely at ease during the examination."

"I shall do so, and I know that Aizza will be very humbled by Ozma's words. She does have an amazing talent for calming her patients."

She handed Aitan the first tablet. "This is the entire MRI scan," she explained. "They used an IV Contrast."

Abana was quiet as he watched the video and as it progressed, she heard him describe each section out loud. "Feet...legs...waist..."

She looked right at him, knowing what was about to be revealed.

"Chest...and now for the heart. Wait. W-w-what is *that*?" he exclaimed in utter confusion and paused the video, giving her back the tablet.

Abana explained, "We reacted the same way when we first saw it, but we had to be quieter as to not startle Ozma during the MRI scan. You will notice that the 'mass' has five organic gemstones: red, blue, yellow, purple, and the center one green."

"Those colors were just like that sphere she created." Aitan recalled.

Abana concurred. "Yes, the video captured it well. Aizza determined that it was not cancerous or some benign tumor. After reviewing the video from earlier, she gave us a SWAG."

"A what?" Aitan inquired with raised eyebrows.

"A Scientifically Wildly Assuming Guess: an organic quantum amplifier."

Abana resumed the video and held the tablet for Aitan to observe.

"Looks like everything else appears human," he surmised after the video finished.

"Yes..." She closed out the video and opened a file titled "Results" before she returned the tablet to him. "Aizza made this presentation after the physical exam, the blood work, and genetics testing results."

"Blood type is AB Negative," he read. "Very rare."

"You remember your human physiology," she quipped.

"Blood pressure is typical for a healthy female. Oxygen levels are good and so are her reflexes. Her weight is well within her height range. All things considered, she's a very, very healthy young woman."

"Now," Abana said, "check the next page."

"Okay, this covers the genetics," he stated. "Aizza emphasized this with bold letters: presence of male DNA found. Okay, she's transgender. Chatulah told me that Ozma said she had been a boy once."

"Ozma said the same to us on the *Golda Meir*."

"What a minute, the next sentence says—"

"Chromosomes are XX, like mine and every other genetic female in my crew and yours. Estrogen levels are well within normal."

"Then explain the presence of male DNA?" Aitan asked with startled confusion.

"Normally, that means a woman has carried a male baby. But she's very much a virgin. In fact, when Aizza asked Ozma about ovulation and periods, she had to be educated on what that meant."

Aitan rubbed his beard as Abana continued. "So either she's lying—even though none of us sensed that—or she's telling the truth. She was once a boy but is now entirely 100 percent female, but has never had a period - the term is amenorrhea.

"Oy."

"I know. It gets even stranger. Check out her TelTest results – the telomere test everyone receives during space duty."

"Telomeres are basically a cap at the end of chromosomes; like plastic tips on a shoelace."

"Correct. They affect aging. There's no comparison to extrapolate Ozma's age, but she told Aizza that she has an 'aged appearance' of a 23 year old," Abana described.

"But her TelTest results say the telomeres are similar to that of a 15 or 16 year old girl."

"Aizza and I both agreed—as did Bethesda and Efren—that Ozma must be incredibly old."

"Conclusion then?"

"She's not entirely human."

There was an awkward pause as Aitan tried to process everything. "Shall we now continue on with our 'known' human: *Yehonatan*?" Abana suggested.

"Of course," Aitan agreed, "but please don't tell me he's some android with microprocessors the size of molecules!"

Both laughed for several moments. "No, he's still very much human," she assured him. "But...well, let's start with his MRI scan. Fortunately, his body was mostly normal," she informed. "except for these two areas." And Abana started a video.

"Okay, this is the scan of the heart," he said.

"Yes."

"The video is progressing slow?"

"On purpose."

"Now I see that," he exclaimed. "It looks like the size of a pearl."

"Again, Aizza determined that it wasn't cancerous. It's another organic gemstone. After the scan, we asked *Yehonatan* what it could mean. He mentioned something called 'hearting' that he and his new wife partake in."

"Wait one moment. Hearting—and a new wife—from where?"

"Remember, he lost his entire family in the Hampton Park Terrorist Attack of May 10, 2029. And we'll discuss his new wife."

"Very well. I do recall the attack, but what is 'hearting'?"

"The best description he gave us is that it allows a couple to share their hearts and thoughts on a quantum level. Normally, it's done with right hands to hearts and a kiss. He and his wife discovered, quite by accident, its quantum entanglement properties when they hold their right hands over their *own* hearts allows them to achieve almost the same thing."

"Regardless of the distance," Aitan added, "if my quantum mechanics is correct."

"Exactly," agreed Abana. "And in light of that, Aizza believes that the gemstone acts as a quantum transmitter and receiver. However, there is an aspect of hearting that *Yehonatan* was eager to state - an unintended consequence."

"And that would be...?"

"It prevents consummation. In his own words: 'My wife and I wanted to try to have a baby and we had the most romantic bath possible to start - we were hearting before we could try anything more than kissing.'"

"Does everyone use this 'hearting'?"

"He said very, very few actually do. Ozma and her beloved and chosen companion, Dorothy, were the first to use it." Abana noticed Aitan's raised eyebrows. "Aizza asked Ozma about her relationship with Dorothy and the description was one of romantic friendship."

Abana sensed his wariness. "Let's go on with the last MRI scan. I know it's been a lot to absorb, so for this one, you'll notice it's actually a recording from Aizza's point of view." She hit play, holding the tablet for him to watch.

"It's just the face and head..." he began. "What is on his forehead? I can see the slight outline of an 'O' and a..." But before he could watch any more, something popped up on the screen:

לא אומר כלום

"Say nothing." Abana declared. "Every time the MRI scan reached his forehead, we'd briefly catch a glimpse of some kind of mark and then every monitor would display the message. Every. Single. Time."

Completely shocked, Aitan remained silent, mouth slightly open. "Let's go on with the rest of the results," he finally requested after several moments.

"All right." She handed him back the tablet.

"Here 'goes," he commenced, reading out loud, "blood pressure good, oxygen levels nominal, reflexes spot on, weight is in a healthy range for an astronaut, blood type is... AB Negative. What are they, related?" he quipped, raising his head and looking at her; Abana enjoyed the laughter with him.

"Next page," he announced.

"Yes, the genetic testing results – and before you review them, we actually do have data on *Yehonatan*. Ever since the recovery of the *Haley*, the Southern Republic's Space Exploration Corps provided the ISA the full DNA records of her crew. The reasoning was that if bodies were ever found, they could be identified. We could have never imagined the past 24 hours, but, having said that, Aizza was able compare the May 1, 2030 data to what was tested today."

Nodding, he remained silent as he read over the results. Finally, he handed the tablet to Abana.

"The telomere results were fascinating," she said. "They've stayed the same."

"But I am curious as to why he hasn't aged since he's been here – it's nearly 15 years later."

"Perhaps it's because of his close proximity to his friend?"

"That's as good a guess as any," Agreed Aitan,

shrugging.

"What did you think of the changes to his ACTN3 gene?" she quizzed. "Aizza was interested with that, as it affects the alpha-actin-3 protein found in skeletal muscles."

"I want to see the results. Aizza took notes regarding him and stated that he had gained incredible speed and didn't know why. Since it also can lead to bursts of power, I think I'll have him and Brian do a mandatory workout together."

"Very clever."

They became thoughtful. "To be sure," Abana contemplated, "this is *Yehonatan's* world, but I would say it's not his home anymore."

"It would also seem that it's neither his female friend's home *nor* her world."

"They don't belong here," both said at the same time.

"But what are we to do with them, Abana?" he wished to know. "They're survivors."

It was at this moment that Abana changed her mind regarding the second tablet. "On that note, Aitan..." She paused to emphasize the point. "No...no," she declared, shaking her head.

"What do you mean, 'no'?" he asked, quite confused.

She picked up the second tablet and gently tapped it against her leg. "Let's go to the Adjunct. I was going to let you review Arial's findings on this, but I've decided that it's better you see them for yourself. Because Aitan, they weren't running away from *anything*!"

"I don't understand."

"Welcome to the club; neither do my crew and I. That Bravo was on a programmed flight plan which was an orbital mapping mission. They were intercepted, Aitan, as they orbited a...habitable planet!"

Abana noticed his entire face light up as if he'd realized something and had become excited with its amazing possibility.

"Oh yes!" she acknowledged out loud.

Having said enough for Aitan to contemplate, she smiled as he directed the train to make haste to the Adjunct station. *Yes Aitan, a habitable planet with cities and civilizations!* her heart cried, and it took all of her self-control not to blurt out that revelation.

The Adjunct Station

As she and Aitan emerged from the multiple airlocks leading from the train and onto the expansive floor of the main hangar, Abana smiled. She had much to be proud of. Her crew had been working non-stop ever since they had landed; the *Haley's* Bravo had been offloaded from her ship, the remaining fuel had been extracted and placed into secure containers, the fuel cells were emptied, and the spacecraft was then carried into the hangar via robotic cranes.

Size-wise, the main hangar was somewhat bigger than an American football field while its backup, the auxiliary hangar, was a little smaller. To access the lunar environment, there were several airlocks for the crew; one for lunar vehicles, and then the main hangar doors themselves. Those doors were actually three separate gateways that worked together: an outer door made of lunar titanium (manufactured at Base Netanyahu and brought to the site) where the segments would fold away or link together for an air-tight fit. Then there was the central door, which was made of melted lunar regolith and constructed on-site. These were staggered and would roll away similar to an aircraft hangar on the earth. Finally, there was the inner door, which was made of material what was used in inflatable spacecraft. Each hangar also utilized several inflatable doors as a way of creating zones to limit total exposure to the lunar vacuum.

Because there was already an ISA Bravo craft in the main hangar, the *Golda Meir's* crew knew which zone was required and they activated its inflatable door. First, extendible rods were locked into place to create support and then air was pumped into the structure. As it was filled, the whole door slowly descended, guided by its far left and right rails and the rods which formed a type of gate.

Once done, the outer door was rolled away and the inner one deflated – this one sank to the floor as plates were laid over to protect it (when inflated, its pressure formed a natural seal against the ceiling of the hanger). Finally, the central door rolled away and work commenced to bring the long-lost Bravo inside.

As for the rest of the Adjunct Station, there was Facility 1 and Facility 2. Facility 1 contained tool shops, spare equipment, clothing issues, and storage of nearly every known consumable needed for space flight. Its total size was just under the auxiliary hangar's. Both hangars were directly connected to it, and right off of Facility 1 was Facility 2. Facility 2 held the living quarters, showers and bathrooms, meeting rooms, classrooms, conference rooms, medical bay, exercise room, and galley. It had two levels with the meeting rooms and classrooms all on the second. Each section was self-contained when it came to ventilation and air.

Abana led Aitan to where the *Haley's* Bravo had been hoisted and they were met by Arial, Blith, and Brian. Several tables had been set up with various instruments from the Bravo for display.

"Aitan," Abana said, "you briefly met my Networks Officer and Navigator yesterday: Arial and Blith."

"Yes, I did. *Shalom*, Arial. *Shalom*, Blith."

"*Aleichem Shalom*, Aitan!" Arial and Blith replied as one.

"Not going to say *Shalom* to me, Aitan?" Brian quipped and everyone enjoyed a laugh.

"Now, for the more serious matter at hand," Abana commanded. "Arial and Blith, you'll describe what you discovered and use this portable holographic terminal to display the results. Brian, you'll then explain what is happening to the *Haley's* Bravo."

"What we have here," Arial began as Blith operated the holographic terminal, "is the *first* flight plan that was logged on the Bravo's systems." A mock-up planet was displayed as a scale model of the Bravo flew around three times and then returned.

"That isn't the one you mentioned to me," Abana stated.

"No, we found this one once we had copied *everything* over," Arial explained. "We'll need to ask *Yehonatan* what that one was about. They basically flew over the same point while in orbit, requiring fuel to adjust course to do so."

"However, the surveillance data produced some fascinating images," Blith added and Arial nodded in agreement.

"Yes, we will have to have *Yehonatan* explain that. Now, for the one you discussed with me," Abana requested, observing Arial and Blith as they followed her order.

The holographic terminal displayed not a mock-up planet like before, but an actual planet with continents, islands, and seas. A scale model Bravo was shown orbiting the planet as it rotated in the display.

"This is what I told you about, Aitan," Abana said. "The Bravo's flight plan was for an orbital mapping mission 290 kilometers from that planet you see."

"That's not a placeholder?" he asked, referring to the planet.

"No, that's a composite image of the planet they mapped," Abana explained.

As Aitan shook his head and rubbed his beard, Blith spoke up. "The data was verified just before they were intercepted. From what Arial, Brian, and I could detect with our version of the Battlespace program, there are cities and civilizations in various stages of development."

"Brian also observed some images of massive sea life that the program had tagged for further review," Arial informed. "And some massive storms - hurricane size."

Abana watched as Aitan took everything in. It was some time before he made his thoughts known. "Then my theory about them being survivors was wrong. Secondly, if I am to understand this data, we are looking at the very first exoplanet that is not only habitable, but has civilizations. Finally, what about this Bravo?"

"Correct on points one and two," Abana concurred. "As for the last, Brian..."

As requested, Brian brought forward a piece of the Bravo's flight systems and opened it up for Aitan to look inside.

"Everything inside is corroded!" he said in surprise. "That shouldn't be since those chips are rad-hardened. (radiation-hardened)."

"We know," Brian answered. "All of the data had been copied over when I went inside to check on the cockpit – everything was dead."

After a few more moments of silence, Abana thanked Arial and Blith for their work and requested that Brian follow her and Aitan to the ISA's own Bravo parked some 30 meters away. "Brian," she asked once they were about halfway there, "how much did my crew tell you about the medical results?"

"Aitan, when do you want Jonathan and I to have a workout together?" he replied with a wide grin and both Abana and Aitan laughed. "I have to admit that when Doctor Dayan explained what the ACTN3 gene did, I figured we'd be having a 'test' sometime soon."

"Okay, so no secrets were kept," she joked. "How good is your Hebrew then?"

"*Al ha-panim!*" (*Really bad*) he blurted out the double-meaning Hebrew slang but chuckled as well. "I'm guessing y'all are wanting to know if I understood that Hebrew message that appeared."

"Yes, and did you?" she quizzed.

"Keep your dadgum mouth shut!" he proclaimed in his pitch-perfect southern accent. It produced the desired results from the other two.

"I accept the Southern Republic's transliteration." Abana snickered.

"So do I," Aitan added with an equally large grin.

"But on that note," Brian said, "I'm glad you two are here; last night, after Jonathan and I finished catching up on current events, we fell asleep hard. I woke up sometime later to use the head—I mean the water closet—and I noticed a faint, soft green light coming from the same place where the scan briefly displayed that mark before the message."

Abana covered her mouth with her hand. "You didn't say anything to him, did you?"

"No. I wanted to bring it up to you both."

"*Todah Rabah*!" She and Aitan gratefully exclaimed together as they all arrived at the other Bravo.

"Good thing we all keep the outside the same color," Abana remarked, referring to the ISA and the SRSEC (Southern Republic Space Exploration Corps).

"Yes, but isn't some bean counter back in Jerusalem going to complain about a missing Bravo worth tens of millions of shekels?" Brian rightfully wished to know. "I understand what you're getting at: transfer all of the data to this – and I'm assuming you will get Jonathan up to speed on this newer model of Bravo."

"True. Abira and I will train him. These Mark Four models come with a built-in simulation mode."

"And as for explaining the loss," Aitan said, "Abana and I will simply tell them the truth – under the highest security classification." Abana nodded in agreement. "The *Haley's* Bravo will be returned; nothing is left of its original electronics and storage, so the mystery continues, but the last piece of the missing spacecraft is at least recovered. What the politicians do with this revelation is all up to them."

Each placed a hand on the ISA's Bravo and pondered what was on their hearts.

"When Abana and I were in the train discussing the exam results, we both agreed that those two don't belong here," Aitan thought out loud.

"Yes," Abana said. "This may be *Yehonatan's* world, but as we have discovered, it's no longer his home. And it's neither Ozma's world nor her home."

"But that begs one question, then. Doesn't it?" Brian asked.

Abana was the one to speak it out loud: "Why are they here?"

The Garden

It was very, very late and Chatulah was understandably tired as she sat on the platform. Sipping her favored grapefruit-flavored sparkling water, she oversaw Ozma zipping around with the push-reel mower. The nearly silent *snip-snip-snip* of its blades were soothing and helped settle her thoughts.

You are the most unusual woman I have ever met, she thought of Ozma. *You may not be the best help, but your heart is in it. At least you sympathized with me as I told you about my great-grandmother's people.*

"Okay, Ozma!" she yelled as Ozma completed the last section to be mowed. "Go ahead and return the mower." She pointed to the shed. "Then come on over here."

Ozma did what was asked and then bunny-hopped over. "This is fun!" she said, taking advantage of the moon's 1/6th gravity.

"Sure is!" Chatulah agreed. "I've got a cold bottle of this sparkling water waiting for you. Go ahead and take a running start and then jump." She watched Ozma undertake the stunt.

"Here I go!" she shouted as she leaped up. Chatulah knew immediately that Ozma had misjudged and quickly grabbed a leg before Ozma flew over the platform entirely. With a thud, Ozma landed on top of Chatulah and the two collapsed into each other.

Ozma was a deep shade of red, in utter embarrassment, and initially Chatulah was too – in anger. However, it soon passed and suddenly, she snickered. Then a snort. Finally, she couldn't hold it back any longer and Chatulah was in full belly-laugh mode! It broke the ice and Ozma laughed at herself as well.

"Here, it's my favorite type." She offered Ozma a bottle of the water. "I make it on demand here at my little desk. It's grapefruit-flavored – enjoy!"

Ozma did with gusto, only to release a small belch. She blushed.

"Yeah, the fizzy will cause that," Chatulah explained. "I sometimes drink that when my stomach feels sour." She too gave a little belch after a long swig.

"Chatulah," Ozma began after she had finished, "how could anyone have done that terrible thing to that young mother's child?"

"I know," Chatulah answered with downcast eyes. "My great-grandmother was good friends with her too."

"Did that mother...?"

"No, she was killed soon after."

"Oh..."

"Yeah."

Both women were quiet as each pondered the day's events, the long hours of work performed, and the prospect of even more.

"Come, let's go shower and then get some sleep. We have another full day tomorrow," Chatulah recommended. "I can say more about my great-grandmother's people tomorrow and how they were thrown out of their land.

With a slight jump, both got to their feet and headed to the showers. Later that evening, Chatulah brought the picture to bed with her. There, she studied it for some time until the soft purring that descended from her roommate above caused her to fall into a deep, fulfilling slumber.

7ᵀᴴ OF ADAR, 5805
(FRIDAY, 24 FEBRUARY 2045)

It had been a long, difficult train ride with no food, no water, and nowhere to relive themselves. Several times, the train had to stop, but the doors had been bolted shut so no one could leave. It was also terribly cold, and many passengers had died before they arrived at their destination.

There was no rejoicing once the train officially stopped. Everyone had been brutally rousted from the rail cars as dogs growled and guards barked out orders in an unknown language. It was dark too, with an overcast sky that made it difficult to see. Separated, her metalworking husband had been forced to go left while she, some other mothers, and a large group of children were directed right. There had been no time to say goodbye.

At 19, she was also the eldest daughter—the she bari —and in her large extended family she had been responsible for their meals, caring for her younger sisters and brothers, and general cleaning. All of that had ended when they were rounded up. She, her daughter, and her husband had boarded one train while the rest had been taken a few days earlier.

She tried desperately to calm her crying two year old. The poor little one had become dreadfully sick during the *journey and her head and body burned to the touch. Several women next to her started to wail as they were were led by guards who wore a skeleton-like head affixed to their collars.*

"Beweg dich schneller!" the guards ordered, using their rifles to push the crowd forward. By now, the group had become mud-splattered and her ankle-length skirt had also become heavy from the rain that had begun to fall. She felt polluted.

Onward she trudged along, trying so hard to comfort her daughter. The muddy ground stuck to everyone's feet like thick porridge or overcooked stew. The pitiful cries from the children added to everyone's misery and even she began to sob.

They finally reached a building and men with clubs and whips urged them to enter through a door. The wailing reached a crescendo as they were pushed forward into a grayish brick room. Strangely, they could feel heat radiating from somewhere close by.

Suddenly, from another part of the structure, a man rushed in screaming, "Kein Giftgas mehr! Töte die Frauen! Verbrenne die Kinder!" A door was opened, showing the burning ovens within, and the door behind them was shut.

A man with a whip grabbed her daughter as she was violently pushed to the floor. In horror—in utter, absolute horror—she witnessed the poor child thrown alive into the open oven. She screamed hysterically, "na...na...na..." (no...no...no...) in her native tongue, and her body exploded with pain as multiple clubs beat her.

Crack...crack...crack... Through her bloodied eyes she saw other mothers being shot and they fell to the floor with heavy thumps.

She began to lose consciousness as several clubs bashed her skull and she could feel it splitting open. The screams of the children being burned alive were the last thing she heard as she sensed being lifted.

The flames devoured her body and all became oblivion.

Ozma was crying uncontrollably. The tears rolled off her face as her heart and soul weeped together. It was as if she was standing in an immense white room that extended for miles in every direction. It was completely quiet.

"Why? Why did this happen?" she grieved out loud.

There was no answer, but then, as before, from out of nowhere, 'a still small voice' spoke and her heart, soul, and mind heard it clearly: "Ask for her forgiveness."

"Why? What have I done?" Ozma yelled back.

Silence.

"What have I done?"

"Done what, Ozma?"

She finally awoke; Chatulah had asked the question. Her roommate was standing on the ladder, gently wiping away Ozma's tears. "You were crying and talking in your sleep."

"I...it was a nightmare." Ozma's voice was hoarse and Chatulah offered her a cup of water – which she gladly accepted.

"Can you recall anything?"

"Pain and heartache," Ozma replied. "That's all I can remember right now."

"I understand."

Ozma suddenly sat up in bed with a hand over her mouth. "Oh, Chatulah, I've woken you up too early."

"That's okay, Ozma," Chatulah replied with a soothing, calm voice. "However, I've been thinking..."

"Yes?"

"Today, at 4:53 in the afternoon, is the beginning of our Shabbat – the day of rest. Since we're already both wide awake now, let's continue where we left off and work as much as we can. For lunch, we can have some grilled fish and enjoy the fruit and dates from the Garden. The cooks have sandwiches for the crew here in case they need to work late – or early," she explained. "Besides, it's been my experience that work like this is good for a troubled soul."

Ozma didn't need to think twice. "Let's do this!"

**Adjunct Station
ISA's Bravo0530
("O Dark Thirty")**

Jonathan yawned as he followed Abana and Abira around the ISA's—soon-to-be counterfeit SRSEC—Bravo. He'd been loudly roused from his slumber by Brian and the rest of the systems engineers. Once he had been dressed and escorted out of the room, Abana thrust a sandwich at him along with the tablet he currently held. The sandwich was quickly eaten during the train ride and washed down with a juice concoction made of fruits and vegetables from the Garden. The little trip had also provided an opportunity to be briefed – his own Bravo a total loss.

His fingers softly brushed the skin of the craft as he walked and once they had strolled entirely around it, he listened intently to his trainers.

"Fortunately," Abira began, "the outside looks similar." She waited for him to nod before she continued. "Our crew is working on getting the SRSEC symbols and numbers stenciled. Arial and Blith are close to having everything copied over from the imaging and flight logs' backups."

"The inside is what matters the most," Abana added.

Jonathan nodded in agreement as he glanced at the tablet and read its specifications out loud. "The frame is now entirely lunar titanium and I see the bottom is now at one-inch thickness versus the three-quarters of an inch on mine. The top is a half inch over all. It's built like a tank – figuratively."

"The main engine systems are 40 percent more powerful than your first generation Bravo, so this one's literally like a lifting-body fighter jet," Abana bantered. "It's even got a laser cannon installed!"

Jonathan's response was raised eyebrows as he noticed both instructors maintained poker faces. "I'm going to check the inventory—"

This Point in Time

"Just joking!" Abria stopped him.

They all laughed for several moments before continuing.

"Craft manifest states it has five micro-communications satellites in the payload bay," he declared.

"They were part of an early lunar network and have been refurbished and upgraded. Since the Portable Capsule Communicator takes only a third of the space as yours did, you'll also find six portable satellite terminals and 12 satellite phones stowed – all with video and text in addition to voice," Abana explained. "Just need a source of reliable power."

"That is available there," he replied. "Now regarding the propulsion system," he continued. "Without refueling, the Bravo can accomplish five sub-orbital flights. The Orbital Ascent Engines can all be programmed for duration in addition to the amount of thrust, allowing for variation in orbital missions."

"The makeup and composition needed to refill them is found on that tablet you're holding as well as the Bravo's own system's folder," Abana informed him. "The main engine can handle a wide variety of fuel too. And before I forget, there is an emergency ascent feature."

"Storage is all DNA-based now. Wow, that's a lot of bytes to use up!" he quipped. "Electronics, surveillance suite, and the flight systems are all obviously 15 years more advanced. Well, now...it has a built-in simulator mode utilizing the cockpit windows as a virtual display." He was genuinely impressed with the latter.

"If you're a pilot, you can learn to fly the Bravo," Abira confidently stated and her boss smiled in agreement.

"I'm guessing you both have been waiting for me to discuss the last feature this Bravo has over mine: a third seat!"

His trainers laughed. "Fortunately, the compartment cover for it is identical to what yours has so it also makes a great way to carry additional gear," Abana described. "Up to 250 pounds worth, and trust me, you'll have lots of extra goodies."

There was a wide grin on his face upon hearing this and he became quiet for several moments with a faraway look in his eyes. "You all have been most kind," he finally said, placing the tablet briefly aside while reaching to unlatch the pilot's door.

"We'll run simulations right up to the start of the Shabbat," Abana let him know, "and then right after the end of the Shabbat tomorrow we'll take the Bravo on a couple of flights. We'll just keep on training to pass the time while you and Ozma are here."

He simply nodded.

"I miss them," he barely whispered loud enough. "My wife and new family over there."

Abana placed a hand on his shoulder and spoke comfortingly. "Aitan and I both agreed that this may be your world, *Yehonatan*, but it's no longer your home. And it certainly isn't Ozma's."

His face showed appreciation at her words. "Thanks, Abana. And you too, Abira – heck, the entire crew of the *Golda Meir*."

"Our pleasure, *Yehonatan*." Abana acknowledged.

"I just wish I knew *why* we were here, Abana."

"We all do, *Yehonatan*. We all do."

Ozma and Chatulah
The Garden – Aquaculture Room

Ozma listened intently as Chatulah recounted how the aquaculture room was constructed. There was opportunity to do so after Ozma had helped retrieve water for Chatulah, and the "gas chromatograph" she had mentioned needed time to "analyze the samples". They were standing on a metal platform.

"The walls and floor are made from the same type of lunar concrete that was used in creating the garden structure. Then, the original crews sprayed a thick, water-tight insulation. You can see that's why the walls have a bumpy texture." She pointed and Ozma nodded in understanding. "The floor was covered with a special resin as well. The same process was done for the other two compartments. The crews then installed the water and electrical lines, fiber optic cables, and the ventilation."

As Chatulah paused, a large school of the fish swimming around caught both of their attention for several moments and they silently watched them. "This..." Ozma pointed to the large pool of water.

"Yes," Chatulah said. "This is basically a large, oval, rigid, above-ground pool with thin lunar titanium sides. The pool itself is composed of multiple layers of fiberglass and structural comb and ribs – the team assembling it actually had several technicians from Israeli pool companies work on it because of their experience."

"It's very big," Ozma commented as she looked over the entire pool.

"Yes," Chatulah agreed, nodding. "It's fifteen meters long by six meters wide, and one and three-quarter meters deep. It can hold over 120 thousand liters of water. The bottom is sloped so water and waste can obey gravity and flow through the filter system. The platform we're on is about a meter above the floor and goes completely around the pool. And there are four different locations to step up to it – one on each end and two along the side facing the sliding entrance doors."

Ozma followed Chatulah back down to the floor and they ended up at one end of the pool. Chatulah took a knee as she pointed to numerous pipes and a large box. "This is also the same on the opposite side," she first explained. "The filter system has two pumps; one will run for 24 hours and then the other will take over."

Ozma's fingers grazed over the large pipe that was connected to the bottom of the pool and the pump. "What does it do?" she asked with a genuine curiosity.

"The pump draws the water out at a constant pressure." Chatulah became animated; she was in her element. "It then feeds that water into the waste accumulator." And she pointed to another large container behind her. "Technically, it's a drum filter and this is where that waste collects and we have to remove it. We can use it as fertilizer or dispose of it."

"I also see three pipes going off that accumulator," Ozma observed. "One has 'To Vertical Gardens' written on it and another states 'To Duckweed'. The last one says 'To Reclamation'."

"Very good!" Chatulah praised. "I'm glad you noticed those. That waste water contains nutrients that can be utilized, and we direct it to the Vertical Gardens located in the other two compartments to be used as a liquid fertilizer *and* to water the plants."

"And what is 'duckweed'?" Ozma asked with raised eyebrows.

"A high-protein water plant that we use for feeding our fish – which we'll be doing soon enough," Chatulah told her. "Now this large tank on the platform is water for the pool." She walked up to the platform with Ozma right beside her. "Notice the pipe labeled 'Raw Water Intake'."

"Raw water?" Ozma inquired, somewhat confused.

"That comes from melted, purified lunar water before it gets made into drinking water for the rest of the station. We keep it at the same pH level in the pool – which ideally should be an eight."

"Could you explain what 'pH' means?" Ozma asked.

"When we get to the monitoring station, I will," Chatulah replied. "The water then runs through a series of pipes similar to a hot-water-on-demand system that the showers use. So now the water is at the same pH level *and* the same temperature range. It then runs through this trough, so follow me." They stepped back up onto the platform and walked to the side of the pool nearest the wall.

Ozma noticed that the trough ended at a miniature waterfall. "This is all part of the pool as well?"

"Yes indeed," Chatulah answered. "First, the water passed through the trough because there are powerful UV—ultraviolet—lights that are used to kill any microorganisms that could infect the fish. Before the water finally enters the pool, flowing over the waterfall adds oxygen to it – what we call aeration. Those three fountains floating in the pool do the same thing."

Ozma nodded in appreciation and observed the waterfall for several moments. Looking down, something caught her eye and she walked from one end of the platform to the other. Extremely curious, she got down on her stomach and leaned over to examine the structure: a long, pool-length rectangular box with pipes running into it with one running up to the waterfall.

"You've discovered our water reclamation system," Chatulah explained with a wide grin as she sat down next to Ozma. "Remember that third pipe which was labeled 'To Reclamation'?"

"Yes, I do!"

"Not all of the waste water is used for the vertical gardens and the duckweed. The remainder goes through this," Chatulah stated. "There are several steps that the waste water goes through before it's reintroduced into the pool: there is a protein skimmer with an ozone, a type of gaseous oxygen, sterilizer, then the water continues on into the carbon-dioxide stripper, on to the biofilter, and finally ensures the pH level and temperature are within an acceptable range."

"Does that water also go through an ultraviolet trough?"

"I missed saying that – good catch, Ozma!" Chatulah quipped. "The pumping system that brings the water up to the waterfall has an integrated UV operation that accomplishes basically the same thing."

"What happens if anything goes wrong with the water reclamation?" Ozma inquired. "I see that the platform we're on has a space of about my fist between the two."

"Excellent question," Chatulah acknowledged. "I'm impressed that you've thought this whole thing through. Fortunately, look behind you and down."

Ozma did as she was asked and pointed to the objects that lined one side of the platform. "They look like door hinges."

"Very good. The platform here can be swung up just like a door to allow access and there are brackets that connect to the wall to ensure that it doesn't fall back and smash someone's head!"

"I bet that can hurt."

"Oh, you'll see more stars than being on the surface."

"Oh, no," Ozma realized, "that's happened to you?"

Chatulah just winked and patted her head, which produced some soft chuckling. "Careless," she recounted. "I had it balanced and I had just taken off my hard hat to wipe the sweat off my brow. Things happened too fast, but my brain and head registered the movement rather slowly. I guess it could have been much worse had the platform been fabricated from heavy steel instead of the lightweight aluminum alloy. Okay, enough of that! Our fish need to eat, so please follow me to those columns on the other end..."

Chatulah got there first and pointed to a metal platform with a ladder between the two columns. "Go ahead and very careful jump up to the top but keep your hands close to the ladder," she instructed.

Ozma did so and quickly reached the spot. She immediately noticed a bubbling fountain that had numerous blue hoses coming off of it as well as two pipes, which continued on to opposite identical green-covered circular basins. Ozma came closer to one and examined it. The water was covered with pea-sized green material that floated on the surface of the water. She observed it flowing from the pipe into a clear bottle of sorts and noticed the bubbles of air it produced.

Squatting, she looked under the basin and noticed a brown hose coming from the center – which was first connected to a gold cylinder. There were also four square pads that gave off a soft light. Another blue hose ran along the bottom of the top basin and in a manner similar to the pipe above, the water flowed into a clear bottle, producing many bubbles. The water was still and again the entire circular basin was covered in the pea-sized green material.

Smiling with her curiosity satisfied, Ozma carefully jumped down.

"Describe what you just observed," Chatulah said.

"I first noticed the fountain with the two pipes and then a bunch blue hoses coming off of it."

"Correct. That water is pumped up there and the fountain is a way to add more oxygen. Blue is for color-coding so we can tell what is the incoming water versus outgoing – which are the brown hoses. Gravity brings it all down."

"I noticed a cylinder attached to the bottom of each basin."

"Yes, that is a water flow regulator to ensure the outgoing water doesn't create a whirlpool and agitates the surface."

"I take it the green stuff is the duckweed?"

"Yep! And you'll notice that there is no trough for the water to go through first. We take that water from the waste accumulator."

"The pipe labeled 'To Duckweed' now makes sense," Ozma happily grasped.

"Exactly." Chatulah pointed to a box on the floor with two pipes on one side and one on the other – which led upwards. "This pump is also a collection tank where we add the raw water as needed and then pump it up to the fountain on top. Inside is a paddle wheel aerator and a little heater."

"I noticed the basins are similar in size to the small ponds in the garden."

"They are, and we use those small ponds to grow the fingerlings that will eventually end up in the pool. The shape and size are important too."

"Why is that?" Ozma asked.

"Adult tilapia need about a square yard of duckweed. Because we use the metric system, each basin contains just over three square meters of duckweed. Each column contains nine basins and there are two of them – so we can support 67 adult tilapia from food we grow ourselves using water that comes from fish waste."

"Very clever!" Ozma proclaimed. "Now that I've learned what duckweed is, shall we feed our hungry fish?" she wished to know with a cheerful smile.

"We shall!" Chatulah replied. "Here are a couple of buckets with scoops. Let's feed the fish and then we'll check on the chemistry of our water. So, if you don't mind, grab a bucket and jump back up again..."

15 minutes later, Ozma was standing at the monitoring station after washing her hands. To her right was Chatulah, who held a fish net on a long pole. She was currently observing one monitor that displayed a diagram of the pool and her fingers hovered over its outline

"There are six 'zones' listed on the display?" she mentioned, reading off the descriptions. "Should I touch one?"

"Yes, go ahead," Chatulah answered. "Tell me what you see then."

"Okay, I touched 'Zone 3' and now half of the screen is filled with large numbers and a color scale at one side that has *1* on the bottom and *14* at the top. I also see a little fish by the number *8*."

"Good...good. I'll explain that color scale shortly. Go ahead and read off the numbers."

"The top number is titled 'Temperature' and two numbers are listed with a little circle by them: 83.00 'F' and 28.33 'C'."

"Ozma, what you are seeing is the temperature of 'Zone 3' in degrees—that little circle stands for degrees—for both Fahrenheit and Celsius. The letter 'F' stands for Fahrenheit and—"

"Then 'C' stands for Celsius," Ozma interrupted with a wide grin of understanding. "Both 'Fahrenheit' and 'Celsius' are ways of expressing temperature?"

"Precisely, Ozma! Just a different scale of doing so – as you have perceived."

"Going on," Ozma declared, "the next is titled 'Dissolved Oxygen' and is reading 5.5...m...g...slash big l." She struggled to understand what she was looking at.

"That stands for milligrams per liter. The readings can also be set to show parts per million – they're interchangeable. Let's just say that Zone 3 is well within the healthy range for tilapia. Fortunately, there isn't a risk of having too much oxygen if we over aerate the water. Now, for the last one."

"It says the 'pH' reading is 8.0."

"That's what we need it to be," Chatulah acknowledged. "The pH is measured on a scale from 1 to 14. Without getting too technical, it's a way to measure base and acidic levels. Bases would be like laundry detergent, whereas acids would be something like lemon juice. Water is considered neutral, so it lies at 7 on the scale. Tilapia can manage to live from 5 to 10 in the pH range but 8 is preferred. The color scale with the fish is a quick way of letting us see that everything is fine. Go ahead and press the 'Return' button and select another zone."

Ozma did as she was instructed. "Very similar," she said after examining the numbers.

"To be expected, as we want the pool to be pretty uniform throughout. Go ahead and select a few more."

After she had done so, Ozma was then directed towards another display.

"In your own words, describe what you are viewing," Chatulah prompted.

Ozma carefully looked over the screen first. There were peaks that contained little text boxes with unfamiliar terms and names and along the bottom was a line titled "Time in Minutes". Going up was a line titled "Response". She traced a finger along the bottom line until one peak caught her attention – it was also highlighted. She attempted to say something but paused several times.

"It's a lot to figure out, isn't it?" Chatulah finally asked.

"Yes. I'm afraid I don't know where to begin. I'm so sorry, Chatulah."

"That's perfectly fine, Ozma. We'll simplify this. Something caught your attention – go ahead and point at it."

Ozma did so. "It says that it's 'ammonia'. And there are two numbers displayed. The first one is called 'Retention Time' and its value is 1.958 minutes."

"In Gas Chromatography, retention time is what determines the identity of the sample. The results are matched against a database of known values."

"Now this I can remember," Ozma noted. "It's saying that the concentration is point 001 milligrams over liters."

"We strive to make it as close to zero as possible. Ammonia is a deadly poison."

"Where does it come from?" Ozma inquired. "And why did it show up anyway?"

"A couple of things going on here. Ammonia is a chemical compound comprised of nitrogen and hydrogen. It comes from fish waste. Even though the value is extremely small, we have our particular gas chromatograph's system to always highlight certain compounds regardless of the amount."

Ozma nodded in understanding and traced her finger over several other peaks. "It's a fascinating system."

"Agreed. And a vital one for our aquaculture facility here. Now if you don't mind, press the 'Save' button to make a backup of today's analysis. Then we're going to go walk up to the pool and get lunch."

Some minutes later, Ozma and Chatulah were simply minding the fish as they swam around. Ozma gently swished the net in the water. After a little while, she sensed that Chatulah was troubled. From the corner of her eye, Ozma would occasionally peer at Chatulah. She noticed that she was tense, and her brow was furrowed.

"Ozma?" she asked in a voice barely audible enough to hear over the pool.

"Yes, Chatulah?" Ozma replied.

"Have you ever heard of the Romani?"

Ozma pondered her response. *"I have heard of a great deal of people and creatures from Oz,"* her heart contemplated. *"I know of Ixians, Munchkins, Winkies, Hammer-Heads, Quadlings, Skeezers, Mountaineers, and of course the Nomes, Gowleywogs, and Phanfasms."*

"I have never heard of that name before," Ozma answered truthfully. "So many peoples and creatures after all of these years. I may have forgotten a few, but the name 'Romani' I have never known – you are the first to mention it."

Ozma could tell her answer satisfied Chatulah and she patiently waited to hear more. It took a little while; Chatulah would repeatedly open her mouth to speak and then close it.

"I hope you understand," Chatulah quietly said, "it's very painful to describe what happened to them."

"I do. I really do."

Chatulah smiled somewhat at Ozma's words.

Just then, a small school of fish caught Ozma's attention and with lightning speed, she scooped them up with the net and effortlessly lifted them out of the water. She giggled at how easy it was – the fish wriggled and squirmed in protest. As she hoisted the net high above the water, she observed Chatulah's face light up – though it wasn't with a smile.

"Ozma, imagine that is what happened to my great-grandmother's people," Chatulah described. "This pool would be the land they had been in – ideal with plenty of food and room. Suddenly, they too were removed – one moment wandering around carefree and the next in a land hostile to them. In fact, let's say you just placed those fish into one of the ponds behind you in the Garden. They could live there, but it would be crowded and not exactly friendly."

"Yes, I can envision that." Ozma grasped. "Those ponds don't have much food."

"No, and because my great-grandmother's people were travelers by nature, it was a big change."

"Then what happened?" Ozma inquired innocently enough as she lowered the fish back into the pool.

"Well, they didn't get that option," Chatulah responded, gesturing to the fish as they swam away. "My great-grandmother was 16 when it happened. Very bad men came and took them – helped along by their so-called neighbors. Imagine those fish again."

"Yes?"

"Out of that small group, only one was 'allowed' to live. The rest were placed into a box – where they suffocated. They couldn't breathe the air. And when they were dead, their bodies were thrown into an oven and utterly burned into ash."

Ozma dropped the net in horror and covered her mouth. "How cruel!" Her face became white at the imagery.

Chatulah merely nodded at Ozma's reaction. Both women had become quiet with heavy hearts until their silence was interrupted by a knock as Lenah Shaked, holding a large basket, made her presence known.

"Hello!" Ozma hailed.

"I understand you two were planning on a picnic?" Lenah cheerfully wished to know.

Ozma glanced at Chatulah, who had also looked at her at the same time. Lenah's youthful, innocent enthusiasm was like a healing balm to the despair that had planted itself within them. They answered as one: "Yes!"

Racing to the finish

After lunch, they only had two and a half hours left before the start of the Shabbat. Despite the longer than planned respite, Lenah's cooking and personality had improved their mood and the delicious meal had provided rocket-like fuel for their final task: harvesting tomatoes and cucumbers.

"We've got a great system going here, Ozma!" Chatulah said quite happily. She wore two sacks – one on each side. With Ozma being quite a bit nimbler than her, she followed behind as Ozma picked tomatoes with her right hand and cucumbers with her left. They worked together like a well-trained sprint relay team.

She's really been a great help, Chatulah said to herself as they walked between what seemed like massive, leafy hills of produce. *There's just something about her...* She released a quick smile – which couldn't be seen by her co-worker.

"You weren't kidding about how productive this compartment was," Ozma declared during a brief pause, face dripping with sweat.

"Yes! Now you can see why I was so concerned," Chatulah stated as she wiped her own soaked brow. "I'm guessing this section alone was about four times more than normal."

"What will be done with all of these?" Ozma wanted to know as they began their little rhythm again.

"Lenah and Judah will be doing a lot of canning – especially with the cucumbers. The tomatoes will be eaten and made into sauces and like much of everything else, used in trade and sent away."

Chatulah saw Ozma's smile as she quickly looked back at her and they worked away. Pick, relay, pick, relay. The moments flew by as they knew they were pressed for time.

With a loud screech, the alarm on Chatulah's watch blared and both stopped to admire their hard-earned victory. Grinning, Chatulah patted Ozma's shoulder in appreciation. "*Shabbat shalom,* Ozma! We've both earned our 'Sabbath peace.'"

Ozma grinned and then relieved Chatulah of one of the very overloaded sacks – which Chatulah gratefully thanked her for. They both placed them in a central location outside of the compartment and closed the sliding doors before they returned to Chatulah's workspace.

There was a large hammock set up near Chatulah's desk and she handed Ozma a chilled bottle of sparkling grapefruit water. Both sat and the gentle swaying was soothing. A few pastries were enjoyed between sips. Though smiling, Chatulah remained quiet and Ozma respected her wishes. This continued for nearly a quarter of an hour.

"I know we're both quite dirty." She spoke after savoring the final swig of her flavored water.

"The shower will feel wonderful!" Ozma added.

"Yes, it sure will," Chatulah concurred. "But since we have both cooled down, I wanted to speak some more about my great-grandmother's people. Actually, it's about someone—a man so evil and twisted—that was given the nickname 'the Angel of Death'."

"Did this man do anything to her?" Ozma asked with great concern on her face.

"No, not to her, but the things he did to others— especially the Romani children—I still have horrible visions from listening to my great-grandmother's stories about him. Oh, Ozma, the twins." Chatulah conveyed deep hurt and disgust as she pounded her fists together before she collected herself.

"What was his name?"

Pausing, she finally answered. "His name was Josef Mengele. Let me tell you about him and his demonic ways..."

Amalie's Shabbat

Amalie yawned hard as she watched over her domain. Ever since the *Golda Meir* had landed, she'd undertaken a most important mission: figure out what happened. It was an almost impossible task had it not been for the brief conversation she'd had with Ozma in addition to the one she had just recorded earlier with Jonathan.

"We were on the data verification phase of the orbital mapping mission. The polar orbits were at an altitude of 350 kilometers and once we had completed the last mapping orbit, the flight program instructed the Bravo to expend some propellant to arrive at an orbit of 290 kilometers. Everything was run according to the

programming David had uploaded. I fell into a deep sleep and I'm guessing Ozma did too. Then the alarms systems just went crazy. Amalie, you should have seen it; it was just like the wormhole from the movie – the one Dr. Kip Thorne had created the equations for. It was big too. I'm thinking a mile across."

Standing to stretch her legs, Amalie also pondered his words describing the actual trip through the wormhole. It was late and she was tired. Though physically she wasn't working, her mind still needed some time to settle down.

There had been a lot of mental prowess demonstrated, and the classroom she had camped out in showed it. There was one smartboard that had Einstein's field equations and the Morris-Thorne metric scrawled across it among mathematical notes from Amalie's own thoughts processes.

Two large displays contained numerous open windows – results of her research. Fortunately, the rules for CommCon 1 on the firewall didn't prohibit searches for works related to the matter at hand. Then, there was another smartboard that contained crude drawings of the moon, the Bravo and its discovered altitude, Base Esther, and several large question marks – those represented the whistler and other mysteries that Amalie had noted. Another smartboard displayed a planet, a circle representing the wormhole, and a small scale drawing of the Bravo. Several notes mentioned the altitude of the Bravo in addition to what it had been doing. Added to that, she had learned the name of the planet itself: Oz!

Finally, to show the distances, a smartboard was positioned between the two and Amalie roughly sketched a Milky Way galaxy. Smiling, she sat back down. Off to her side she had an air mattress with sheets and blankets, and the classroom's refrigerator held plenty of snacks and simple meals for her to enjoy with a small microwave to heat them. Abana had also guaranteed Amalie that no one would bother her.

Amalie's eyes had become heavy, so she warmed up a small cup of herbal tea to help quell her mind. Sipping it, she again scanned over her work. A thought came to her and she grinned, playfully tapping her forehead.

"But it's Shabbat," she quietly rebuked herself. "However," she declared, "the rabbis may have said that writing two letters was prohibited..." Amalie walked up to the smartboard of the moon. "There!" she announced, drawing a single circle by the Bravo.

Stepping back, she glanced at the board with the planet. "Entry!" Then, looking at the one with the newly-drawn circle, she pointed at it. "Exit!"

8ᵀᴴ OF ADAR, 5805
(SATURDAY, 25 FEBRUARY 2045)

"Ask for her forgiveness." The 'still small voice' directed at Ozma's heart as she entered dreamland. After a busy day and the start of the Shabbat, sleep had come quite easily. However, for Ozma it was a startling request, as it seemed to come out of nowhere.

She felt like she was floating in a pitch-black void, unable to tell which way was up or down, or even see her own hands in front of her. All was quiet, the air stagnant. Even her heartbeat was absorbed by the all-encompassing darkness.

Again, the 'still small voice' spoke to her. "Ask for her forgiveness."

"Why?" she retorted in a somewhat irritated tone. "What have I done? And just who are you?"

Silence. Absolute terrifying silence coupled with the sensory-deprived, lightless nothing.

Then suddenly, she found herself as a little girl—just over four years old—on a playground. She and her twin sister were giggling as the carousel spun around faster and faster. Other children could be heard laughing as they enjoyed the swings. The sandbox too was enjoyed as castles and imaginary kingdoms were explored and fierce dragons conquered.

It was a pleasant, sunny day with barely any clouds. The adults who watched Ozma, her twin sister, and the rest of the children had ensured they were well-fed and accommodated. Over and over, the overseers—comprised mostly of women—assured everyone they would be with their parents soon enough. In the meantime, they were special guests and were to have fun.

Little Ozma and her sister jumped off the jungle gym at the same time and landed in a pile of dust. Giggling until their bellies were sore, they got up and chased each other around the carousel and then all over the playground. The children enjoyed a recess from their kindergarten and preschool studies.

An attractive, charming man walked up to where a group of children were playing and soon gleeful shouts of "Onkel Mengele" were proclaimed. The man smiled and tousled their hair as he passed out sweets.

He was a slightly built man with piercing brown eyes. His green tunic was pressed and neat, and his boots had been polished to a mirror-like finish. The man's face was shaved and he smiled while whistling a tune. Ozma and her twin sister skipped hand in hand up to him and he gathered them both in his arms. A little toy was produced to each and a small chocolate bar was split for the two to enjoy.

"And how are my beautiful little girls today?" he asked through a translator. The sisters grinned and a little hand from each touched his smooth face. The man laughed and told them it tickled. "Would you two like to follow me?"

Ozma and her twin both nodded and they took the hand of one of the women once he had let them back down. It was a somewhat long trip, but his whistling entertained them. Finally, they walked up some steps and entered a building.

"I will see you again," he informed them through the woman who held their hands and he went off into another room. Ozma and her sister were led into a side room where they received a quick bath. From somewhere inside, music could be heard – similar to *what was played in their preschool on a gramophone.*

Cleaned and dried, the twins donned robes before the woman guided them to a room with bright lights, a table, several carts, and people wearing smocks – including the man. Ozma giggled at the gramophone in the corner.

"You like that?" he cheerfully asked before she nodded.

Ozma saw someone hold a cloth to her sister's face before she too received the same treatment and all went black.

It was quite a bit of time before Ozma regained consciousness. At first it was the nauseating stench she noticed and then it was the excruciating pain that burned throughout her body. The room was dark as her eyes slowly opened. She screamed in horrific agony, which was made all the louder when she heard her sister's wailing.

Ozma tried to move, but she couldn't – she sensed someone up against her.

She started to panic and the shaking only caused the torment to increase. She cried out for her sister and her hands finally touched something; it felt like fine, sticky string.

Back and forth their heads moved, trying so desperately to see one another. The motion only intensified their discomfort. They were crying, screaming, and shaking – they couldn't help it. The two were in shock, suffering inhuman misery.

Chatulah

"This one's going to be bad," Chatulah stated quietly. She had been going over the picture when Ozma's moans became louder and louder, her body thrashing under the covers. Chatulah briefly returned to contemplating the picture when Ozma woke up screaming, sitting straight up in bed. Greatly startled, Chatulah jumped back and dropped the picture, which fell face-down on the floor.

"The pain! I can feel it. My twin...my back..." Ozma choked out.

Oh no, one of those, Chatulah thought as she rushed to Ozma's side.

Skin damp with sweat, she shook, hands waving erratically. "Ozma..." Chatulah tried to say but was pushed back. *The poor girl. I know, I know.*

"Ozma, look at me," Chatulah commanded, grabbing one of her hands. "It was just a bad dream," she firmly told her.

Ozma shook her head in disbelief.

"No," Chatulah softly whispered. She took Ozma's hand and slowly eased it behind Ozma's back. Up and down, the hand was gently stroked against her shirt where stitches would have been. "See?" she whispered over and over. "It was just a nightmare, Ozma." Chatulah caressed a cheek with her free hand.

Ozma wept.

"It's okay. It's okay," Chatulah whispered, holding her close and letting Ozma's tears flow onto her shoulder. "I understand. I really do. It was the twins' one, wasn't it?" The tightened grip from her roommate was all the confirmation she needed and there they stayed for some time.

When the tears ceased, Chatulah quietly spoke up. "I've had those nightmares before, too. My therapist back in Israel called it 'inherited trauma'. It's sort of like post-traumatic stress. What's always helped me..." She stopped and Ozma lifted her head, looking at her.

"What has always helped me is to get outside and just sleep under the stars. The stillness of the air and its coolness settles my mind. Why don't we get out of here and do just that? I'll find another hammock and we can just talk until we fall asleep."

"You've been too kind, Chatulah," Ozma responded, deep gratefulness in her eyes as she held Chatulah's hand in agreement.

"You've been..." she paused, "you've been a good help, Ozma." She stepped down, letting Ozma get herself ready.

As they were just about to leave, Ozma saw the paper face side down on the floor and picked it up.

"Oh, I nearly forgot that," Chatulah blurted out. "It's a picture. A very, very old picture that my great-grandmother drew when she was only eight years old." She took it from Ozma hand. Once folded, she returned it to its the frame and the two headed outside.

Fellowship in the Garden

"Here," Chatulah happily announced once the second hammock had been moved next to the first, "it seems that Lenah baked us some delicious snacks to enjoy – *hamantaschen*." And she handed a plate to Ozma. "She used some of the dates we gave her the day before," she further explained while placing another bag under her own hammock. Both took a bite.

"Mmm." They succulently agreed to Lenah's masterful pastry creation then laughed as one.

"Lenah is such a marvelous cook," Ozma declared, enjoying yet another *hamantaschen*.

"Yes, she is. Both she and Judah are already scheduled to be the chief cooks at Base Netanyahu once their tour here is over." Chatulah gave Ozma a carton of milk to drink. "It's warm, but it's what we call 'shelf-stable' so it's perfectly fine."

"Different," Ozma observed once she had swallowed.

"Yes, it does take a little bit getting used to." Chatulah drank some herself then giggled, covering her mouth with a hand.

"I'm going to introduce you to something we call a *kumzitz*," She suggested and quickly explained herself upon Ozma's look of puzzlement. "It's something my great-grandmother did when she was in the Palmach. It's Yiddish and it basically means to 'come, sit down'."

Chatulah retrieved a tablet and sat back down. A few taps on the screen and the overhead displays burst forth a beautiful nighttime scene. "A *kumzitz* is where we sit around a fire, eat, talk, sing, and just have fun. We can't have a real fire here, but we can have everything else."

Another tap produced soft music.

Ozma listened for a few moments before commenting. "That's catchy. What is it?"

Chatulah's face lit up with glee. "It sure is, and it's my favorite, too – the Israeli Kibbutz Folk Singers. And this one's called *Haleluyah La Olam*." She began to sing along.

Haleluyah im hashir

Haleluyah al yom sheme'ir

Haleluyah al ma shehaya

Uma she'od lo haya

Haleluyah

Caught up in the mood of the moment, she clapped to the beat as well. "Come on, sing after me, Ozma," she cheerfully encouraged.

Ozma wasn't so sure. "Chatulah, I don't even know your language," She protested, but to no avail.

"Just follow my lead." Chatulah playfully grabbed Ozma's hands. "Ready? *Haleluyah*."

Resigned to her fate, Ozma sang along with heart – if not with the correct pronunciation. "*Ha...lay...loo...yah...*"

"See? Not too shabby! *La'olam*."

"*La...o...lam*," Ozma repeated with a growing smile.

"It's fun! *Haleluyah*."

Ozma started getting into it. "*Ha...lay...loo...yah!*"

"There you go – *yashiru kulam*."

"*Yah...shir..u...kuh...lam*."

"Great! *Veha'inbalim hagdolim*."

Ozma dearly tried but all she could do was snort and laugh – as did Chatulah!

"Okay, that one might be tough. We'll finish the last three verses. *Haleluyah al ma shehaya*."

"*Ha...lay...loo...yah.. al...ma..she..ha...vah...*"

"*Uma she'od lo haya*."

"U..ma... she.. owed.. lo...ha...yah!"

"Wonderful! And together now!

"*Haleluyah!*" Ozma pronounced perfectly.

Chatulah clapped happily, her whole face glowing with joy. It was as if all the worry had fallen away. She smiled at her roommate, and it was a genuinely appreciative grin. "That was fun."

"Yes it was!" Ozma agreed.

Chatulah reached under her hammock and retrieved the other bag. "This is beef jerky, compliments of the Republic of Texas." She gave half to Ozma with some grapefruit-flavored water to wash it all down.

Ozma finished her portion rather quickly. "Looks like you were hungry!" Chatulah joked.

"Guess I was," Ozma replied as a small belch bubbled up through her mouth - which caused her to blush and giggle.

Chatulah joined her, lightly ribbing Ozma, who grew even more red. Soon, a snort was released, and then a full belly laugh and both women enjoyed the humor of the moment. After several minutes, the merriment abated and silence returned. "I can tell you're totally calmed down now," she told Ozma.

"Thank you, Chatulah. I've never had a nightmare that vivid before."

"The one with the twins is very hard to get over," Chatulah confessed with sad eyes. "It angers me to no end that there are people who deny this ever happened. That evil doesn't exist." She took a deep breath. "I must apologize for that," she said wearily. "It's something that cuts very, very deep."

There was an awkward pause as they looked at each other. Finally, Chatulah spoke. "I can imagine you'd like to talk until we both fall asleep?"

Ozma's face lit up with a large smile. "I hope you don't mind."

"I more than understand. Well, what would you like to

discuss?"

Ozma didn't take long to answer. "I would love to hear more about your great-grandmother. But first, you mentioned something earlier about the 'Palmach'? Could you explain that?"

Chatulah grinned widely. "It would be my pleasure, Ozma. The Palmach were the elites of the Jewish underground army, the Haganah. This was during the time when Israel itself didn't exist, but the land fell under the British Mandate for Palestine. The name comes from the Hebrew words *plugot mahatz* – strike companies or strike forces."

Ozma nodded and Chatulah continued. "They were established on the 14th of May, 1941 by the higher-ups of the Haganah. The aim was to defend the Jewish community against threats from the Axis or the Arabs. When the British ordered them to be disbanded after the Second Battle of El Alamein—1942 I believe—they went underground. They kept themselves as an organization by working in the kibbutzim."

"'Kibbutzim'?" Ozma inquired with raised eyebrows.

"Plural of kibbutz – communal farms that were established," Chatulah explained. "Each kibbutz hosted a platoon and they were fed, clothed, and housed while providing protection."

"Clever," Ozma remarked and Chatulah nodded in agreement. "One of many ways everything had to be done back then. Nothing was easy and nothing was given to them."

"Now, about your great-grandmother?" Ozma asked with a soft smile that spoke of genuine curiosity.

Chatulah became animated. "I have her very eyes!" she proudly boasted, gesturing to them and leaning in so Ozma could see.

"They're pretty, Chatulah," Ozma complimented.

"Thank you," she replied. "Everyone was amazed when I was born. Great-grandmother was more than pleased when she held me for the first time. She was a feisty woman," Chatulah added. "She also had a 'I don't care' attitude after she survived Auschwitz-Birkenau."

"That was the 'death camp'?" Ozma inquired.

"Yes. She was the only one out of nine who made it – also losing a baby sister whom she loved dearly. And she always shed tears when talking about her, Ozma. The rest were murdered. Sadly, out of all her people who had been sent away to the countries of Southern Europe and then delivered to the camps, only several managed to live. She tried to keep in touch with them and was successful for a while until the last one died in 1963 and her letters were returned."

Chatulah became quiet, staring at the ground with great sadness. Some tears fell as she softly spoke more. "She was really attached to her baby sister, Ozma. When she found out..." She fought back the tears. Ozma gently touched her hand and she calmed. "Thank you." She nodded in appreciation. "She fell into a deep depression and almost felt like giving up and surrendering her spirit to that domain of death. That was until she met Samuel."

"Samuel?" Ozma wished to know.

"Great-grandfather," Chatulah clarified. "He was 15 years older than her and already had a family. *Had*." She made sure to emphasize the word.

"Oh no."

"And Auschwitz, evil as it was, wasn't the most heartbreaking part."

"Really?" Ozma asked, surprised.

"You see, he was a Jewish man from Amsterdam – an architect. He had three daughters and a wife who was pregnant when they got sent to Westerbork – a transit camp in the Netherlands." Chatulah had a fierce look in her eyes; she was full of anger. "Westerbork was built on delusions and lies, all to lull its victims into sedation." She reached out and touched Ozma's hand. "Not only did the place allow people to leave the camp, but there were theater performances, cabarets, soccer fields with teams in uniforms. Inmates were allowed to attend church, work in factories. All of it was a ruse."

She resumed with a faraway look that pierced right through Ozma and into the past. "It was the hospital that really sealed the deal with death, Ozma. Oh, the people were all treated nicely, but in the hospital the finest doctors made sure they were well taken care of. People were often in much better shape after their stay at the hospital than before their arrival. Before they were shipped on a one-way train trip to *sheol* – the grave."

Ozma hung on to her every word. "His wife had complications with the pregnancy and the doctors there not only ensured that the baby boy was delivered safely, but that she had exceptional postnatal care. She and the child were the picture of health when they were shipped out – along with the rest the family."

Ozma placed a hand to her mouth. "All of that just to keep up the Nazis' deception?"

"Yes."

"Oh, my goodness."

"Well, Great-grandmother and Great-grandfather saw something in each other that transcended their different backgrounds. She was kind of like a Ruth to him and he was like a Boaz covering her with the blanket of his heart. He even shared some of his prison bread with her when she hadn't had anything to eat – starvation was another way Auschwitz operated."

Mouth dry, Catulah took a long sip of the milk. "They managed to be among the last of the survivors when Auschwitz was liberated on the 27th of January, 1945, by troops of the Soviet Union. They were married in the middle of the night by a Jewish Red Army soldier – he had hidden his rabbinical background. They then literally ran from that camp of darkness. They had to be careful as they traveled – even after liberation it wasn't safe. She told me they had to be as clever and crafty as cats. They both received grief for having married each other. Great-grandfather was criticized for wedding a 'thieving Romani' and other disgusting slurs."

"After all they had gone through..." Ozma remarked.

"Yes. And when Great-grandmother ran across some

other Romani, she was called 'polluted' for having married a Jewish man. Oh, Ozma, she really let them have it! I still remember her words."

Chatulah composed herself with pride and a wide smile spread across her face as she spoke brave words from a distant past: "Listen, both Samuel and I were polluted by that abode of death and we each had to wear badges of shame – I with the black triangle and the 'Z' and he with the yellow and black triangle for being a 'race defiler'. You have no right to call either of us 'polluted!' None!"

"Bravo!" Ozma concurred. "But what do you mean by 'badges of shame'?"

"The concentration camps made each inmate wear badges for identification purposes. Great-grandmother's was for being a female Romani."

"And your great-grandfather was called a 'race defiler'? What does that mean?"

"Ozma, his late wife was a gentile woman—a Christian—and the 'master race'—the Nazis—didn't take too kindly to the 'wrong' humans marrying each other."

Ozma just shook her head.

"Now, they had been told by some survivors that they needed to travel south and reach a place called Tarvisio, Italy." Chatulah mentioned. "There was a miracle of miracles there."

Chatulah grabbed Ozma's hands and gently squeezed them to make her point. "It was the Jewish Brigade Group! An entire British Army unit composed of Jews! Can you imagine their feelings at that? She told me Great-grandfather had wept tears of joy."

"They stayed with them for about three months. In that time, they received training on all the weapons the Group possessed, and she discovered that she had a 'keen eye through a rifle's sight'. Finally, they were transported by trucks south to be smuggled aboard ships heading to the British Mandate – that was late fall of 1945."

"That was the name of the area before Israel declared its independence," Chatulah said. "She and Great-grandfather were immediately taken by the Palmach and they learned about explosives while passing on what they had been taught. It wasn't long before they were using that knowledge.

"They saw quite a bit of action together. There was Operation Yiftah in Eastern Galilee – 20th of April till 24th of May 1948. They both were wounded during the fighting. Then once Israel declared its independence on the 14th of May, everything intensified. Israel was invaded by multiple armies all dedicated to exterminating the Jews there. Great-grandfather acted as her spotter during the conflict. The things they witnessed, experienced, and heard would freeze your soul, Ozma."

"I can imagine, Chatulah," Ozma said in agreement. "When did the war end?"

"It still goes on," Chatulah blurted out but explained her words. "I mean, the original war was ended with the 1949 armistices signed with Egypt, Lebanon, Jordon, and Syria. However, the struggle continued in the 1967 Six-Day War, the 1973 Yom Kippur War, the so-called 'Land for Peace' deals, children being taught in schools to murder Jews, and even in space in 2045. We always have to be careful." Chatulah sighed heavily.

"What became of your great-grandparents after the original war?" Ozma inquired.

"Well, the Palmach itself was disbanded in November 1948, and absorbed into the IDF. But their ethos and traditions continue to this very day. Great-grandmother declared once peace had begun that her 'days of wandering were over'—except when working her crops—and the only adventure she wanted was the making of babies and raising them! They were blessed with eight children: four boys and four girls. Great-grandfather helped design buildings while they lived at the kibbutz."

"What a fascinating account," Ozma stated.

"Yes, it is! I never got to see Great-grandfather though. He passed around 1985 – 15 years before I was born. And Great-grandmother died when I was five. She drew that picture—which is of the 'one who sent us away'—back in 1933. I was the only one to believe her story too. I've sworn to avenge her and her people if I ever can. She's the one who gave me my nickname: Chatulah." She smiled.

"You mean...?"

"I don't reveal my actual name to many people, Ozma. The nickname is Hebrew for a female cat. It's funny, once I had to serve in the IDF, I joined the Caracal Battalion in her honor – a unit named after the Caracal cat!" She chuckled and Ozma did, too.

"A woman with a nickname for a female cat joining an IDF unit named after a cat! That is funny!" Ozma agreed and both laughed for a bit.

When it grew quiet, Chatulah touched another icon on her tablet. The scene above them became a beautiful star-filled expanse with mirror-like calm water below. It was breathtaking and awe-inspiring. The ambiance speakers broadcasted soothing sounds of the night. It felt like they were both really there.

"Oh, Chatulah," Ozma remarked with absolute admiration. "That is simply gorgeous! Where is it from?"

"It's from the Sea of Kinneret – also known as the Sea of Galilee," Chatulah described. "It's actually streamed from a location back in Israel. Well, not exactly a livestream because the data would take up too much bandwidth between the moon and the Earth. They take a 30-minute snapshot of video and audio, compress it greatly, and then send it."

"Your overhead displays are a fantastic addition to the garden, Chatulah."

"Thank you, Ozma."

"In a way, it reminds me of something back home – a picture that allows me to see anything I ask of it. Except during the times of those purely evil creatures," Ozma added sheepishly. "I can imagine you must think I'm making this up."

Chatulah shook her head and softly answered, "I had a chance to read the report that was given to Aitan. I know this isn't your home or world. I've seen the medical charts and the MRE results. I believe you. But if that 'picture' allows you to see whatever you wish, wouldn't that include Earth?"

"Yes. I often looked on Dorothy when she lived in Kansas."

"Are you the only one who uses that? I can imagine people might get quite mad about their privacy being violated."

"Fortunately, it's in a room in my chambers. You're not the only one to express such concerns, though; General Benjamin said basically the same thing. I don't often use it."

"I see," Chatulah acknowledged. "Now, speaking of 'Dorothy', Aizza Dayan's notes mentioned that you called her your 'beloved and chosen companion'. Since I've done most of the talking, why don't you tell me more about her? When you're done, I think we'll both be able to fall asleep. We can sleep in tomorrow – when we get up is when we get up."

It was a request Chatulah immediately knew Ozma appreciated as her face radiated joy and love. "My most beloved and truest friend. We met as young girls..."

A lonely breakfast

Lenah and Judah Shaked were reading and reflecting over the Scriptures together in the kitchen. When she looked up and noticed a lone individual in the mess, she pointed her gaze in his direction as her husband glanced up as well. They watched him out of the corner of their eyes for a few moments. It was Jonathan, picking at a sandwich while studying something on a tablet.

Several times, Lenah observed him place his hands on his head and then tap the device. She could tell somehow that he was holding back tears by the way he sniffled. Finally, it was too much to just watch and she quietly whispered to her husband. They rose and walked over to the table where Jonathan sat.

"Shalom, Yehonatan!" Lenah said with such a cheery tone that it made him smile back.

"Aleichem Shalom, Lenah and Judah," Jonathan replied.

"Not very hungry, are you?" Lenah asked, trying to make small talk. She knew the answer. "Do you mind if I look at that picture?"

Jonathan slid the tablet over to her.

"Aww! Look, Judah!" she cried with glee. "Was that taken just before your flight?" she inquired of him sitting down in his space suite and the four females around him.

"Yes," he softly acknowledged. Smiling, he described them. "That woman there is my new wife – Princess Betsy Bobbin."

"A princess?" quipped Lenah. "You've married up in your new home!"

He chuckled and began to relax. "She's my 'Angel with the brave, brave heart'," he said with a glint in his eye.

"I can see that," Lenah noticed. "The way she holds herself close to you – her love is true!"

Judah spoke up after he had examined the picture. "It may be 15 years later here, but you've only been there for about six months. Those other girls in the picture?"

Lenah giggled and lightly tapped her husband's shoulder in jest. "Judah! Maybe time works 'differently' over there," she joked. "But my love does have a point. You lost your own family on May 10th, 2029. Are they friends?"

Jonathan grinned. "Betsy and I adopted them." He pointed at the two youngest girls. "That is Anusha," he indicated the darker-skinned girl. "She was brought to Oz from India."

"So Oz is a real place, a parallel world," Lenah remarked. "She's beautiful, *Yehonatan!*"

"Todah rabah, Lenah," Jonathan agreed, nodding. "The other little girl is her 'big sister' Tina. I'll have to explain that: Anusha arrived as a newborn and grew a year every

week until she matched Tina's age of eight."

"So time *does* work differently over there." Lenah laughed and they all joined her.

"For her it certainly did," Jonathan explained. "Tina and her big sister Tara," Jonathan pointed at the taller girl, "are the only survivors from their village." He shook his head in sorrow. "That was due to some really nasty creatures."

Lenah nodded and both she and Judah held his hands. "You miss them terribly, don't you?"

"I do, Lenah. I really do. I just wish I knew why I was here – especially now."

Lenah looked at her husband, as he had been rubbing his chin – which she knew was his way of pondering his thoughts. "Remember *Yehonatan*," he said. "Yah fearfully and wonderfully made you. He knows your every thought – when you sit down and stand up; whether here, or there. By His word the heavens were made and all of the stars. *Psalm 147* tells us that, 'He determines the number of stars and calls them each by name'. You are there for a reason, just as today you are here, 15 years later. You must have faith that you will get back there."

Lenah was happily nodding. "That is right, dear," she stated, glancing at her husband. "The key here is faith, *Yehonatan*! I'm going to read from the *Book of Hebrews* and then I'd like for you to read a portion, please."

Jonathan remained quiet. "Okay, go ahead," he said after a while.

"Good! Now, it says here in *Hebrews 11;3* that, 'By faith we understand that the universe was formed by God's command, so that what is seen was not made out of what was visible.'"

Jonathan concurred. "Isn't Hebrews…"

"Good Jewish literature!" Lenah answered and Judah smiled at her.

He chuckled and acquiesced. "I'll read that portion now."

יא מהי אמונה? אמונה היא ביטחון מלא בדברים שלהם אנו מקווים, ומצב שבו אנו משוכנעים

במציאותם של דברים שאיננו יכולים לראותם.

After he'd scanned the page, Jonathan translated it into English out loud. "*Hebrews 11;1*, and it says, 'What is faith? Faith is full confidence in the things we hope for, and a situation in which we are convinced of the reality of things we cannot see."

"Very good, *Yehonatan*!" Lenah praised. "You are here for a reason and you will get back. You must have faith."

"If I may add something too, *Yehonatan*?" Judah requested.

"Sure," Jonathan answered.

"We all witnessed what your friend Ozma did to heal you. That world she is from is now your home; can you do anything like that?"

"No. I refuse to."

"Then even more so, you must place your faith in the Holy One of Israel. You are from one of the Twelve Tribes. Your faith must never be in what you can do, but in what Yah is doing. Remember the Shema and the greatest commandment: to love the Lord your God with all your heart, soul, strength, and mind," Judah boldly proclaimed.

Lenah added, "And to love your neighbor as yourself. It's a good thing Samson is listed in *Hebrews* for faith!" she quipped.

Judah playfully tapped her side. "And Rahab too, dear!"

Both softly laughed and Jonathan couldn't help but chuckle as well. "I see what you mean about faith," he said. "*Todah*."

"*Bevakasha*!" Both replied.

"Now *Yehonatan*, Judah and I are going to pray over you," Lenah informed him. "And when we are done, Judah and I would like to invite you to our study of *Isaiah*

40."

Jonathan took both of their hands. "I am humbled and very appreciative."

And so they commenced praying.

Reading, reflecting, and realizing

Ozma and Chatulah slowly swayed in their respective hammocks. After they had slept in, an early brunch was consumed. Finally, they settled into a relaxing, cozy routine of simply reading. Ozma used a tablet that Chatulah had lent her, accessing Internet archives via the LFON to the servers at the ISA's Base Netanyahu.

It was bewildering. Nothing could have prepared her for the sheer volume of information – good, bad, indifferent, or useless. To be certain, Ozma easily remembered her earlier lessons from Jonathan about using a tablet, but until she had experienced the rush of browsing for herself, it had all been for academic purposes.

An eager search about Purim led to articles on the Holocaust, which linked to further articles on something called 'democide'. She tapped an icon as each subject popped up and she silently read them.

Democide: a term coined by Rudolph Joseph Rummel, circa 1994. She thought that over. *"The intentional killing of an unarmed or disarmed person by government agents acting in their authoritative capacity and pursuant to government policy or high command.*

"See examples?" the page requested, and she tapped the 'yes' icon. A table was then shown and Ozma's hand flew to her lips in utter shock. The numbers were astounding – almost unbelievable. So was the disclaimer: *numbers based on historical accounts with varying accuracy.*

In her heart, Ozma was grieved. The century that was supposed to have been a Utopian paradise by man's own will turned out to be an abyss of misery and woe. *"World Total 1900 to 1999 262 million."* The numbers scrolled before her, cold and brutally efficient in their simplicity. *"People's Republic of China: 80 million. Union of Soviet*

Socialist Republics: 62 million. Colonialism: 50 million. Nazi Germany: 21 million." There were many others.

Oh Jonathan, my dear brother. Now I truly know the tragedy of your world, she said to herself. "I need to find something else," Ozma whispered out loud selecting one of the bookmarks. It was about videos and as luck would have it, a playlist of cats popping balloons, dogs refusing to get bathed, and cute corgis commenced playing. The entertainment had the desired effect on her mood.

She softly giggled for a while and when the last video had provided its last laugh, Ozma placed the tablet down and got up to stretch. She noticed Chatulah was still on her own hammock, reading a book while quietly speaking what she assumed was Hebrew. Ozma respectfully refrained from any questions until Chatulah took a break.

"May I ask what you are reading?" Ozma wished to know. "I also overheard you talking in Hebrew?"

"Yes, I was. I sometimes do that while I read my Tanakh." Chatulah explained.

"Ah, I see," Ozma understood. "What is a 'ta-nach'?"

Ozma saw Chatulah's wide smile at the opportunity to answer the question.

"Tanakh is actually an acronym for the Hebrew Bible."

"The Bible? you mean 'The Great Book of the Mortals'?" Ozma asked.

Chatulah was taken aback by Ozma's words. "I must say that I have *never* heard it described that way, but yes, it is indeed great because it's God's Word."

"I see. And you mentioned that it's actually an acronym – Hebrew I presume?"

"Very much so, Ozma," Chatulah happily acknowledged. "Let me expand upon that and you can repeat the Hebrew with me. Sound good?"

"Yes!"

"Very well. Now 'Tanakh' comes from the three traditional subdivisions of what we call the Masoretic Text. And then we take the first Hebrew letter of each of those to create the acronym. Ready? The first is called *Torah*."

"*Taw-ruh*," Ozma repeated.

"Good," Chatulah encouraged. "The *Torah* is called the 'Teaching' and they are the *Five Books of Moses*."

Ozma's eyes widened with recognition. "I remember that name! Moses is the Great Lawgiver!"

"Oh ho! You do know something about us," Chatulah said.

"Yes, he was handling everyone's disputes by himself until his father-in-law told him he needed to delegate people who were trained in the law to help," Ozma explained.

"Moses could be stubborn," Chatulah added with a chuckle. "Jethro was an excellent consultant."

Both softly laughed. "Now for the second part," Ozma requested.

"Yes," Chatulah obliged. "Going on, we have the 'Prophets' which in Hebrew is called *Nevi'im*."

"*Nev-e-eem*," Ozma pronounced.

"Not bad!"

"What books are in that?" Ozma wanted to know.

"We list them as the Former Prophets such as *Joshua*, *Judges*, and *Samuel*. Then the Latter Prophets, such as *Isaiah* and *Ezekiel*, and finally the Twelve Prophets who include *Hosea*, *Joel*, *Zechariah* and *Malachi*. The Twelve are also known as the Minor Prophets. Which reminds me, the name *Mikra*—the Hebrew for 'that which is read'—is another word for the Tanakh."

"Very interesting, Chatulah. *Todah Rabah*?".

"Very good, Ozma, *Todah Rabah* is indeed thank you. *Bevakasha*!"

"That means 'welcome' – I learned that from Jonathan. So, the final portion would be?"

"That would be the *Ketuvim* – the Writings."

"*Ke-too-vim*!" She eagerly repeated.

"Well done, Ozma! Now those are also divided into four sections: history—*Ezra* and *Nehemiah* for example—and even some prophecy—*Daniel*—and the poetical books—*Psalms* and *Proverbs*—and finally the *Megillot: Scrolls*. That would also include *Esther*, which is the one I'm currently reading because Purim will be celebrated soon," Chatulah added.

"*Esther* and Purim; Jonathan talked quite a bit about that."

"Rightfully so, Ozma. Queen Esther is one of the greatest Jewish heroines of all time. She risked her very life to save her people - for such a time as this God had placed her in that position."

Ozma pondered her next question and she hesitated for several moments. "She risked her life to save her people - the Jews. Could they have been rescued through slavery?" Immediately, Ozma realized how deep that request had cut: Chatulah's face displayed great anger. "I-I'm sorry." But then, she saw Chatulah's face soften and instead of anger, she now appeared sorrowful.

Chatulah took Ozma's hands and spoke soothingly. It was not what Ozma had expected. "You can be so incredibly naive, Ozma." Ozma even nodded her head in agreement. "Look at me," she said. "You cannot beg for slavery when one-way riders of death are bearing down upon you with swords in one hand and spears in the other. Orders had been sent calling for the utter destruction of her people - orders that could not be rescinded. So, orders were issued after Esther's immense bravery that allowed her people to protect themselves. Instead of annihilation, there was celebration because their enemies had been killed and the man responsible for starting it all—Haman—was hung on the very gallows he had constructed to execute Esther's cousin Mordecai."

"Chatulah?" Ozma was meek. "Please teach me about Esther."

Still holding her hands, Chatulah wholeheartedly began. "Ozma, it would be my absolute pleasure. Come, I will sit next to you and you can read along. My Tanakh has both the Hebrew and the English translations."

"*Todah*, Chatulah," Ozma said with humility and appreciation.

"*Bevakasha*, Ozma," Chatulah softly replied as she took up the seat beside her. "Let's begin. *way'hiy Biyméy áchash'wërôsh hû áchash'wërôsh haMolëkh' mëhoDû w'ad-Kûsh sheva w'es'riym ûmëäh m'diynäh....*"

Baruch HaShem

Amalie stood at the front of the classroom with her displays and smartboards. With an ample amount of expended mental horsepower and reading, she'd had her "Eureka" moment, or in the case of her ethnicity, her Baruch HaShem—Praise God—realization. She had solved the problem of the Whistler signal!

One smartboard showed the planet labeled Oz with a circle to indicate the wormhole and the scale Bravo with notes for what it had been doing: an orbital mapping mission; its orbital altitude at the time of the entry into the wormhole and the date—November 3rd, 2030—labeled the diagram. Amalie had also included a screenshot from the orbital mapping mission of one of the storms the imaging had captured. Next to the word 'Entry', she'd roughly sketched an atmospheric whistler.

The middle smartboard again had the rough sketch of the Milky Way Galaxy, but through it, she had drawn lines showing magnetic waves traveling through a tube representing the wormhole. Finally, the third smartboard showed the Bravo at its discovered altitude, the word 'Exit' by the circle, then their date – 5th of Adar, 5805 and February 22nd, 2045. Along these representations of the moon and Base Esther, a symbol for the *Golda Meir* had been added, and the previous question marks had been blocked out with notes. Finally, and with several exclamation points around it for emphasis, another whistler had been drawn – right by the word 'Exit'.

She stood off to the side of the last smartboard with the equations and notes. The entire crew of the *Golda Meir* had been invited, and ever since they'd mercilessly ribbed Jonathan for his flying skills. In solidarity to him still wearing his spacesuit—the flight with the ISA's Bravo had only recently concluded—Abana and Abira donned theirs as well. She had also invited Aitan and whoever else he might deem necessary. All they had to do was simply wait for that group to arrive.

"So after all of that training and all those simulations, when it came to landing..." Abana paused to keep her crew in suspense, "he landed a half meter off center!" she concluded with a grin and a chuckle.

"Aww! Oh boo!" the rest responded, slapping Jonathan's shoulders in jest.

"And I told him, not bad for an amateur!" Abana finished, which elicited even more raucous laughter. Amalie enjoyed that joke as well

Even Abira contributed to Jonathan's verbal beat down. "And get this," she began with the widest smile possible, "he had the audacity to request The Blue Danube during the landing sequence!"

Amalie observed him starting to protest but he stopped mid-response. "You're not going to win this one, *Yehonatan!*" Abana stated and even he laughed.

"Look, he's blushing!" Amalie heard someone shout and the rowdy fun continued until Aitan and his group finally arrived.

"*Shalom,* Aitan and crew!" Amalie greeted for everyone to hear.

"*Aleichem Shalom!*" Aitan replied and quickly introduced the members of his entourage. "I've brought along Brian Ascot—most of you already know him—and Abra Ozeri and Abner Joachim, my systems engineers. And these twins are Ashu and Asher Dahan: my communications technicians."

Amalie shared a quick wink with Abana, who covered her mouth to hide a grin.

"Welcome everyone!" Amalie then got to the point of the meeting. She started at one end of the room with the smartboard depicting Oz. "We know from the recovered flight logs of the original SRSEC's Bravo that *Yehonatan* and Ozma were not escaping from any emergency - rather they had been conducting an orbital mapping mission using polar orbits. After the last orbit had been completed, the Bravo then performed a preprogrammed maneuver to adjust its altitude from 350 to 290 kilometers for the data verification phase.

"From our own analysis of the imaging data, we noticed some very large weather systems – corroborated by *Yehonatan's* observations. The date on the Internal Systems Clock showed November 3rd, 2030 – nearly six months after the *Haley* itself had crash-landed."

She pointed at the circle representing the wormhole. "At some time during the data verification phase, at an orbit 290 kilometers from the surface of Oz, that Bravo encountered a wormhole. *Yehonatan* told me that it looked just like the one from the movie that used Dr. Kip Thorne's equations. And so they entered the wormhole." She then walked the path out – simulating their journey. "This tube is a crude representation, but for this discussion it's enough. The Bravo traveled through that wormhole until..."

She jumped, rather easily in the moon's reduced gravity, right to the smartboard with the moon. "It came out at a location some 290 kilometers straight above Base Esther. That is where we later discovered and rescued *Yehonatan* and Ozma.

"Some things that we know about wormholes: there is an entry and an exit; they can connect two points in different universes—in this instance between Oz space and Earthspace—and they can also connect two points in different times." She spread her arms out with one pointing at each of the entry points drawn on the smartboards. "Over there in Oz, the Bravo was showing a date of November 3rd, 2030. Here it was the 5th of Adar, 5805 – or to make an easier comparison, the 22nd of February, 2045.

"That explains the operation of the wormhole and how *Yehonatan* and Ozma arrived here. But, that was only a part of the mystery. The whistler –"

At that, Ashu spoke up, nearly repeating his previous explanation word for word. "That would be an electromagnetic wave propagating through the atmosphere that occasionally is detected by a sensitive audio amplifier as a gliding high to low frequency sound." He breathlessly added, "And these electromagnetic waves originate during lightning discharges and are usually in the frequency range of 3000 to 30,000 hertz. That's why the base stations picked it up on the VLF receivers."

The group's entertainment at his expense didn't bother Ashu, but his brother Asher did playfully smack his shoulder for interrupting. For her part, Amalie just softly laughed along. "Our resident experts have provided the scientific explanation for a whistler!" She announced. She repeated, "The whistler," and let the group ponder that.

"The Bravo wasn't broadcasting over its radio. The whistler was detected out of the blue for a duration of 115 seconds. Then, without any warning, it ceased and wasn't heard any more. That was the great mystery." Amalie opened up an article dated September 3rd, 2015 and maximized it so everyone could at least read the summary.

She pointed at it with a wide grin and eyes that shone like stars. "This article was the key and my *Baruch HaShem* moment." Amalie played a brief video animation that described how the researchers from the Autonomous University in Barcelona, Spain had created a magnetic wormhole, connecting two regions of space.

"The experiment created a tunnel that transferred the magnetic field from one point to another while keeping everything undetectable. For our purposes here," Amalie said as everyone started to grasp the implications of the discovery, "when the wormhole opened over Oz at an altitude of 290 kilometers..."

This time Asher chimed in "I get it!" he shouted excitedly. "Whistlers can be no more than 25,484 kilometers from the Earth. The wormhole transferred the electromagnetic waves of the whistlers for the duration it was open and the signals ceased when the wormhole was closed." Both brothers were nearly jumping up and down.

Amalie sat and released an audible *whew* as Abana came up to shake her hand. "You've earned your newest PhD!" She proudly proclaimed. "Well done."

Amalie merely nodded and smiled. Then, as all became quiet, Amalie rose to her feet again and spoke some final words.

"As to *why* the wormhole was opened up," she said firmly yet humbly, "I'll leave that one, for the rabbis."

9TH OF ADAR, 5805
(SUNDAY, 26 FEBRUARY 2045)

"Ozma, do you wish to learn about Deborah?" Chatulah asked before they had laid down to sleep.

"Is that another heroine?" Ozma wished to know.

Chatulah had softly said yes while yawning, so she began to read. It wasn't long before Ozma's eyes grew heavy and she entered dreamland.

"How long have I been walking?" she asked herself aloud. It seemed to have been hours upon hours in the confused state of time that dreams often inhabited. The land she traversed was hot and arid – but not totally a desert, for she witnessed plants and trees here and there. Fortunately, her clothes were flowy and light so the heat was not as burdensome. It was a hilly country too as she had hiked up and down several of them.

Off in the distance, Ozma spotted a large palm tree. Quickening her pace, she could see two people sitting as she drew nearer. By the way they dressed, Ozma could tell they were women. When she arrived, she was waved in closer to join them and then she too sat down. There they stayed for some time – the stares from the women in front of her pierced Ozma's heart and soul.

There was complete silence except for the wind rustling the palm tree fronds. The two women were dressed differently, yet both exuded a strong leadership that was also balanced by the humility behind their expressions. Ozma's heart discerned the one to her right as being Queen Esther. As if confirming her thoughts, Esther smiled and nodded.

Ozma was in awe of the Queen's appearance. From her own study with Chatulah, she had learned about Esther and the words had only partially done her justice. She possessed a natural beauty, which was magnified by her incredible heart.

Her gown was made of the finest silk chiffon with long sleeves and exquisitely embroidered gold thread. The bodice consisted of priceless gems of all kinds. Her skin was soft and perfumed; the scent was like nothing Ozma had ever detected before. Behind her was a cloak make of royal purple. Her necklace and crown put Ozma's own circlet and headpiece to shame – as if they were cheap toy knickknacks.

The woman next to Esther remained silent but pointed a finger upward and behold: a live diorama presented itself. Ozma watched with fascination as images of people being harassed by a cruel foe ran by. They cried out and then the woman was visited by a man with a sword. She watched as the woman accompanied him and his troops into battle. Ozma shuddered at the opposing army's strength and numbers – which included hundreds of chariots. She heard the sound of battle as if she were right there, at the foot of a mountain.

Ozma then witnessed the very weather turn against the enemy and the once-imposing chariots became bogged down. The man and woman's forces then destroyed that army until not a single soul was left standing. The leader of the opposing army ran away and eventually staggered into a tent, which was guarded by another woman. Soon after, Ozma heard a tent peg being struck by a mallet and the man was led inside by the other woman.

Together, the man and woman serenaded her with a great song of praise.

The woman next to Esther then spoke. "I am Deborah,

a mishpat of Israel. For forty years, my people had peace because I was faithful to the Lord God of Israel. You have just seen what my people had endured and what we had to do to free ourselves." Her voice was firm.

"Deborah," Esther said, "is one of the most remarkable women of all time. She is known for her courage and wisdom - renowned on her own merit and not because of others. She was a judge - a 'mishpat' in Hebrew. She was a poet, a prophetess, and a military strategist."

Deborah, who wore a colorful robe and shawl over her head, had bracelets that clinked as she moved her hands. Ozma could tell they were made of a shiny metal. Deborah also wore earrings that reflected the sun as she spoke.

"A great leader is humble," she informed Ozma, who also observed Esther nodding in agreement. "And a great leader is humble enough to never be a warmonger, yet wise enough to know that there may be times when you have no other choice but to yield the sword in order to protect your people."

Ozma blushed because of her own failings.

"You are here for a reason," Deborah explained.

"Which shall soon be revealed to you," Esther interjected, "but for now..." Both women gazed upward.

Ozma was used to it by now as the 'still small voice' spoke to all. "Ask for her forgiveness." Initially, Ozma was irritated and her face began to show it. However, this time both Esther and Deborah placed their fingers to her lips with raised eyebrows, their gazes piercing Ozma's heart.

Again, they gazed upward as the 'still small voice' declared once more. "Ask for her forgiveness." Her lips sealed by their fingers, Ozma's heart attempted to cry out, but it too was somehow silenced.

Finally, the 'still small voice' wistfully repeated, "Ozma, ask for her forgiveness." This time, the directness of the Voice gave Ozma reason to pause and ponder. Her face displayed not haughtiness, but sadness *and concern.*

At this, Israel's Heroines began to fade away with the wind until only their eyes remained, imprinting themselves onto Ozma's soul.

She awoke peacefully. The room was dark and quiet, and Ozma could hear Chatulah's breathing as she slept. "I want to go home." Ozma quietly whispered, "Please, I just want to go home."

She received the answer just before she faded back to sleep.

"Ask for her forgiveness."

The Mess

It was early, but not too early as Aitan sat and enjoyed his favorite hummus and a hot mug of herbal tea. The mess was mostly empty too; other than him, it was just Lenah and Judah, who were cleaning the kitchen. Traditional Jewish music played softly over the speakers.

Once the Shabbat had ended, he enjoyed a nice two-hour long session on one of the bike-machines in the exercise room. Prior to his breakfast, he had completed the required one hour of cardio and one hour of weight resistance training. Feeling hungry, he had foregone his shower to enjoy breakfast first and remained in his gym outfit. However, he was also waiting for some news to validate what he and Abana had talked about regarding *Yehonatan's* "modified" genetics – in particular his ACTN3 gene. He had the perfect hard-charging workout buddies in Abner and Brian to conduct the tests.

Aitan didn't have to wait long before he overheard their loud voices as they arrived and sat down opposite him. The pair still wore their exercise clothes and each held a plastic bottle filled with a vanilla-colored, frothy liquid.

"Breakfast?" Aitan inquired.

"Yep, a good protein shake." Brian answered. "Very enjoyable during the train ride back."

"The Adjunct has a nice exercise room." Brian and Abner nodded in agreement. "You guys are always free to use it."

"Yes, but once the *Golda Meir* crew is gone, that's still a large empty place," Brian retorted. "Kinda creepy if you ask me."

"Would make for a great B horror movie, too," quipped Abner and they all laughed.

After a few moments of frivolity, Aitan pushed his bowl of hummus aside and leaned back in his chair. "And what do my workout warriors have to report?"

"Well," began Brian, "the ladies were wrapping things up."

"Abana does have a tight ship and a sharp crew," Aitan said. "So I take it the rest of the workout was just you three then?" He sipped his tea.

"Yes, just us," Abner acknowledged.

"Okay...?" Aitan asked, stroking his chin.

He saw both men across from him take a quick glance at the other before Brian commented first. "Jonathan's a fast runner."

"Tell me something we didn't already know!" Aitan smirked.

"Oh, just *how* fast?" Brian joked.

"That was half of the test, so yes."

Abner answered for Brian this time. "He had Olympic speed – the treadmill's auto-protect had to kick in."

Aitan was incredulous. "And was that a sprint?"

"Both," Brian and Abner replied quite seriously and Aitan's face displayed confusion.

"Amazing speed with unbelievable endurance," explained Brian. "We've got everything on video if you want to see for yourself."

"I'm quite certain those with the highest clearances would appreciate that. I'm fine though – I believe you guys."

There was a pause for a few moments.

"The strength workout went as expected," Brian finally

said. "Until he got mad."

"What do you mean, 'mad'?" Aitan quizzed.

"Well, he didn't turn green, become big, and smash things if that's what you're concerned about."

"Ha ha. Funny one, Brian."

"Compared to us, he was decently strong – and that was while he was calm," Abner stated.

"A poet, I see," Aitan joked. "We kind of expected that as the ACTN3 gene can give bursts of increased speed or strength when someone's under stress. Now, what did you guys do to make him mad?"

He waited for their answer as they grinned at each other and with raised eyebrows. Aitan barely heard Brian's muttered reply. "Abner...smacked his knee."

"Hey, I tripped! Really, I did!" Abner confessed and for his part, Aitan pursed his lips and crossed his arms.

He snickered as he witnessed the two pranksters smack each other's shoulders. "Told you he wouldn't fall for it," Brian said.

Aitan finally smiled. "Okay, just explain to me what exercise station he was at and what the results were."

"It was the chest press," Brian started.

"Good, good."

"We started him at 185 pounds of resistance."

"How did that go?"

"He managed pretty well," Abner answered.

"Then Abner and I took turns – needed to increase the settings," Brian joked. "Too little to get a good workout."

"I see humility is your strong point, Brian," Aitan bantered. "I take it Abner went right after *Yehonatan*, and then you were using the machine while Abner 'tripped'?"

"Basically how it went down," Brian replied. "He was ticked! I told him to do several sets to work his anger out."

"Did you increment it or just leave the settings at a

higher amount?"

"I set it to be quite high," Brian recalled.

"He did three sets of ten easily," Abner described. "Darn, it was impressive. Very, very impressive."

Brian concurred, "Dang impressive, Aitan."

"Okay, so what was it set to then? 225 pounds of resistance?"

Both men pointed their thumbs upward, indicating he had to go higher.

"300?"

Still, the thumbs shot up.

"400?" he asked, becoming more skeptical – yet he was in awe at the same time.

"Keep going," Brian encouraged

"Over 500?" Aitan challenged, leaning over the table to emphasize his disbelief.

"Yes!" both replied.

"I had set it to 530 pounds," Brian explained matter-of-factly.

Aitan whistled his amazement and shook his head. "You two weren't kidding."

"Yeah, it was an interesting workout for all of us," Brian commented.

"Where is he right now?" Aitan inquired.

"He's at the Adjunct, and he's probably already showered and had some breakfast," Brian conveyed. "He said he was going to be explaining the imaging to the *Golda Meir* crew shortly after."

"Hmmm...I can't be there for that, but you can be, Brian," Aitan affirmed. "Abner?"

"I've got some network settings to look over. Station audits for you?" Abner asked.

"A little of those, but mostly about what has been going on – video conferences with higher-ups at Base Netanyahu," Aitan responded. "Though I'm going to be reviewing the inventory of goodies we have for him and Ozma, so that will be after his briefings."

"That reminds me," Abner interjected. "We need to replace the routing module on Base Station Five – it's older than our facility."

"Oh, that's right," Brian declared. "I can take the lunar truck to get that done and we have the best guy to help out since he's the oldest and it's 'his' era: Jonathan."

They all chuckled, but Aitan spoke up. "That's harsh, Brian."

"Well, the moon *is* a harsh mistress," Brian retorted.

"You like Robert Heinlein?" asked Aitan, impressed.

Brian gave him a wide smile as an answer.

"I'll be monitoring the whole operation," Abner announced.

"Good. Very good," Aitan praised. "And before I forget, Brian please see me before you go over there. I have a secure tablet that contains some 'interesting' results of what they found from the *Haley*."

"Gotcha, boss," Brian answered.

Just then, a loud crash startled them and they all turned towards the kitchen. It was Asher, blushing and looking quite guilty.

"Asher, what are you doing?" Aitan called. Asher opened his mouth, but nothing was disclosed.

However, Aitan caught a quick movement out of the corner of his eye and in moments he knew he'd been setup – his bowl of hummus had been swiped by a running Ashu.

Realizing he'd been outwitted, he added his own laughter to the snorting and guffawing released by Brian and Abner.

Now we know

I just can't wait to get home, Jonathan said to himself as he collected his thoughts before his presentation to the crew of the *Golda Meir* and Brian. The new Bravo was off to the side, completely ready to be loaded into the upper bay of the *Golda Meir* – no more training required. Nearby, a long table held all the "goodies" that were going to be given and stored in the third passenger's compartment once he had a chance to inventory them. Finally, his briefing would utilize three large displays: one held the imaging from the first orbital flight, the middle was photographs of his family, David, and Trot, and those from his team's exploration along the Swath of Restoration in Munchkinland. Finally, the last one depicted the completed orbital mapping of Oz.

All eyes were on him as he sat down on a stool with a serious expression. Just as he was about to begin, someone from the group blurted out, "It's Rabbi *Yehonatan*!"

That broke the ice, and everyone enjoyed the comedy at his expense – even him.

Once the snickering had died down, he began. "Please, any of you can stop me during this briefing to ask questions. I've seen things over there that I can still hardly believe exist. I don't think anyone could have imagined Oz to be a parallel world with a mix of human and not-so-human, beings. And I know that I'll probably be jumping around a bit, so my apologies beforehand. Having said that, let's begin with the knowns: the *Haley* left Charleston harbor on May 10th, 2030, and you all know of our brief visit at Base ANZAC – these are a matter of record the Southern Republic made known. It was when we were en route to our training location in lunar orbit that we encountered a portal – which is our best guess. Once we were able to review our flight logs on the table display, Allen—Chief Johnson—noticed we had pushed four times the normal flight speed."

"That was a substantial increase!" Abana commented.

She was joined by a question from Aizza Dayan, the *Golda Meir*'s Physician. "What happened to you and the rest during that time?"

"We lost consciousness," Johnathan said. "Anyone who wasn't secured in their seats when the *Haley* aerobraked didn't make it. I was very lucky, as my belt had failed to unlatch – I had been trying to help our Navigator prior to the *Haley* entering the portal. The flight logs recorded this as an anomalous energy storm. As for who caused our aerobraking, I'll defer to Amalie's comment: ask the rabbis."

"How many were killed?" Blith wished to know.

"Our new XO, Jason Martinez, our Navigator, Matthew Orion, and our Environmental Chief, Jay Menvy. Jason and Matthew had their necks broken, but Jay...Jay had been in the Crew Space working out," Jonathan sadly recalled. "His passing was...rough."

He stood by the display showing the first orbital imaging. Selecting the optical layer, he zoomed in until the *Haley's* position could be seen. "The automatic system took control – thankfully. We landed next to this city. Well, it was quite a long skid, as you can see from the imaging."

"*Yehonatan,*" Amalie requested as she stood, arms crossed and a hand against her chin, "how did the *Haley's* hull handle the stress of the landing? And the reactor and propulsion systems?"

He smiled, having recalled the all-nighter that Allen and his crew of Emilio and Hector Gomez had pulled as they reviewed the entire engineering system's status logs. "When we returned the day after landing, we all walked around to see if anything was badly damaged," he answered. "The titanium hull more than survived the crash on land versus a normal one on water."

"And the reactor and propulsion?" Amalie inquired again, which brought about some light ribbing from Abana.

"First and foremost, always the Chief Engineer!" Abana quipped and he and the rest laughed with her. Jonathan noticed her blushing and he smiled.

"The good news from Allen, Hector, and Emilio was that the reactor was itself fine," he stated.

"So, the 'bad news' would have been the propulsion system?"

"Very much so, Amalie," Concurred Jonathan. "The

diagnosis from the logs was that our sudden acceleration was brought about by a huge increase in heat transfer efficiency. And it was the reactor heat exchanger to the propellant tubes leading to the rocket nozzles. The engines came offline because the sensors simply melted," he further explained.

Amalie's shocked face spoke volumes. "The temperatures required for such a thing to happen..." she pondered out loud.

"I know," Jonathan acknowledged. "The tubes were fused."

He observed Amalie's sad shaking of her head.

"*Yehonatan,*" Abana interjected, "are you aware that the *Haley* was eventually found in orbit around Ceres? Me, Arial, and Amalie were part of the recovery crew. During your time here, have you had a chance to read the email that Commander Jon Kryton wrote about the *Haley*?"

He quickly gave his answer. "Yes, I read it just before this briefing - thanks, Brian." Brian gave him a thumbs up. "I guess my ping6 command is what got everyone's attention."

"Indeed, *Yehonatan*. It was picked up by Project Ozma IV's radio array!" Arial proclaimed.

"Yes, I chuckled at that name," Jonathan agreed.

At that time, Blith stood and pointed at the middle display. "*Yehonatan,*" she said, "could you explain these pictures of you, David, and those other people?"

Thoughtful, Johnathan paused, stepping closer to study David's picture. "That woman next to him is Princess Trot and she is his new wife in Oz. You want to talk about two people who were just waiting for the right time and place to meet, that would be them. They became Ozma's security detail."

With his back to the group, he placed his hand on the display where Betsy was as if trying to caress her cheek across time and space. He was quiet for some time and fortunately, everyone behind him was respectful of that.

"That's your new family over there, isn't it?" he heard someone ask – it sounded like Arial. He shook his head "yes" in response..

"They're beautiful, *Yehonatan*," she commented.

"Thank you," he replied after he had composed himself. Turning around, he pointed at Betsy. "That is my Angel with the brave, brave Heart. Her name is Betsy—Princess Betsy Bobbin-Kohen—and she is my beloved wife."

Everyone clapped in congratulations.

"You've come a long way from May 10th 2029, *Yehonatan*," Abana remarked. "We all grieved when we heard the news of that terrorist attack."

Deeply grateful at her words, Johnathan shed a few tears. "As for the other three girls," he explained, "because of what I can best describe as a form of magic called 'hearting', Betsy and I cannot have children – we adopted."

His words caused guffaws from Mahri and Davette, who snuggled up to each other.

"*Yehonatan*, love is its own special kind of magic," Mahri quipped and everyone else—including Brian—laughed.

He blushed deeply, which didn't help matters.

"Look, everyone! He's blushing!" Davette announced. "That must be some very strong love!" Even he snickered at his own expense.

"I needed that comic relief," he exclaimed after they had calmed down. "Okay, having explained that…time for children is normally the same time as here in Earth-space. However, that young lady is Anusha." He pointed to the olive-skinned girl. "She's from India and our best guess is that she came from a village in the mountainous regions there. It looked like her home suffered a massive flood too. Ozma has something that enabled us to discover that."

Arial ran to a nearby table and grabbed a tablet. Tapping away, she sat back down. "For those who may not know, Anusha means 'a beautiful morning star', and I think I may know where exactly in India she came from."

Jonathan waited; he could tell Arial was excited. "I'm accessing the archives from Base Netanyahu," she added. After about five minutes, she literally jumped up to him, showed him the tablet, and then shared what she had discovered on the middle display.

"Pandukeshwar?" Jonathan asked as Arial showed them an article from the *India Times* of early summer 2030.

"Yes!" she answered. "They had had a devastating flood, and your time line would coincide with what happened. Now, this is what made me remember." She scrolled to a picture of a mud-encased couple.

It was a somber scene: a man with a woman over his shoulders with her arms outstretched. They looked like a rough statue.

Arial grabbed his hands. "Relatives were able to identify them, *Yehonatan*! They'd just had a newborn baby girl. You see, that child was never found!"

"Oh wow!" He gasped – as did everyone else. "Anusha's birth parents."

"Everyone can take a break," He announced and watched Arial return to her seat and continue scanning the tablet, utterly fascinated by the article – a few tears were shed.

He was handed a fruit and veggie smoothie by Aizza and enjoyed it while walking around the Bravo. The ladies from the *Golda Meir* had made it look identical to his old one. He reached out, fingers skimming the surface several times. Then, he headed over to the original, placed a hand on it, and kissed its surface. "Thank you, old friend," he said quietly. "Now the last missing piece will be returned."

They were all ready for him to continue once he had walked back. Standing again at the middle display, Johnathan gestured to Anusha. "Arial made a good point: Anusha was a newborn when she arrived in Oz. In fact, she still had her cord stump. Yet, as you can see in this picture, she looks similar in age to Tina, who is eight." He pointed to the other little girl standing by Anusha. "From what Ozma guessed, the transit from Earth to Oz must have imparted some kind of energy to Anusha and she grew a year every week. Trust me, we were just as surprised as all y'all," he joked, noticing their wide eyes of disbelief.

"Anusha would have these bands of energy weave all through her as she grew," he recalled. "It was during the transition from year one to year two that Anusha imprinted Tina's age – they had been sitting next to each other and the energy flowed through Tina as well. Well, Anusha grew that way for the next six weeks until she matched Tina's age. As for Anusha, she has Asperger's Syndrome."

"Didn't little Rachel have that too?" Abana asked.

"Yes, she did," he affirmed. "She has an affinity for math, maps, and patterns. In fact, she had one heck of a meltdown during Ozma's birthday celebration. Out of a Throne Room filled with hundreds of objects, Anusha found one that had been placed not quite correctly – just over half a centimeter off. She was...quite insistent on the layout being wrong." He rubbed his cheek as he remembered.

"Tara is the oldest and was a member of an elite military unit," he said, gesturing to her and Tina now. "In fact, Tara arrived with her commander, General Gittan-Nora, and Lady Glinda just after we crash-landed in Oz. The hull was still hot, so after things had cooled and Allen had engaged the automated gangplank, Tara had been one of a couple fellow soldiers who helped DOC get me out of the *Haley*."

At that, he paused and sighed deeply.

"DOC and the rest," he said softly, almost too quiet to be heard. "And that is how I'm going to explain what happened to them." He walked over to the display that contained the original imaging and selected the radar layer. "I hope everyone understands this is difficult for me because the tragedy could have been avoided if Glinda and Ozma had asked for our help. There we were, a 21st century spaceship crew with the *Haley's* technology, our computers, and even the Bravo, and they thought we had brought beings with us – incredibly evil beings that had no remorse or pity."

"What do you mean, 'evil beings', *Yehonatan*?" Abira asked, still sitting. Wanting to know the answer as well, the rest all nodded at her request.

Johnathan scrolled the radar layer until a threadlike yet solid line appeared and he zoomed in a little bit. He also went to the other display with the orbital mapping images and selected a view that included Oz with the surrounding deserts. It was the optical layer, and he magnified the image until the edges of the deserts touched the edges of the display.

Heading to the middle display, Johnathan selected a picture from the Swath of Restoration and also one that presented glass made from fused desert sand. In the distance stood massive glass towers with the sun's light reflecting every which way. Both pictures occupied an equal amount of viewing space. He borrowed a laser pointer from Arial so he could more easily answer Abira's question.

"What you are seeing," he directing the laser to the thin line on the radar layer, "is what was called the Magic Barrier. It was put in place by Glinda per Ozma's request to make Oz invisible from the outside."

"Somehow, anything from our modern era must have been able to see through it?" Blith asked.

"Correct," he replied. "When we arrived in May of 2030, the barrier had been in place for 120 years." He then used the pointer on the image of Oz and traced all around it. "So for all that time they couldn't be seen. However, that barrier was probably the mother of all unintended consequences and here's why: on a quantum level, it trapped something – something everybody has to deal with and is always there." He let the group hang on his words.

Danni nearly jumped from her seat with her hands to her head. "No, no, no. I can't believe they ignored something that simple." He merely shook his head in response and let her continue. "We know from *Genesis* that every inclination of man's heart is evil from his youth, and *Jeremiah* clearly says that the heart is more deceitful than anything else and morally sick."

Everyone's expressions became concerned.

At their logical conclusion, Johnathan spoke up. "The very thing they—Glinda and Ozma—had wanted to protect Oz from an external invasion which very nearly led to their destruction from the perfect *internal* enemy: the trapped evil thoughts that all humans and half-humans have. Those thoughts collected and grew, eventually doubling in size, and would have continued to do so had we not shown up. It was the ideal, evil storm."

"How could they have even considered you as the cause?" Abana wanted to know.

"Several reasons, Abana," he answered. "One is that they were living a complacent life and had absolutely no clue about the storm of pure evil on their doorstep. From what we were told later, except for fog, they couldn't have been able to see them with Ozma's Magic Picture. Two: the *Haley's* arrival shocked them, and thirdly, they never considered the possibility. They believed that they had conquered evil. Also, something that David's father-in-law—Bill Weedles—said made perfect sense. Give me a moment to remember." He paused to think. "Ah, now I've got it. Here it goes: 'When the glass is falling, you can't blame the ship for the storm that was already there.'"

"So basically, here is how I see this." Abira stood with everyone watching her. "That barrier was put into place to make them safe from any external invasion. But unknown to them, that barrier trapped every evil thought within. Those thoughts grew and grew and eventually doubled until you and the *Haley* crash-landed. So they must have seen you guys as a sign of sorts to attack, but they were not as big as they could have been?"

"Yes," he simply declared, waiting as Abira indicated she was to speak some more.

"In simplest terms, you guys flushed them out."

"Long story short, yes," he concurred.

The group released a long, sad sigh, and Blith softly asked, "Those beings are what killed Allen, Emilio, Hector, and DOC?"

Johnathan paused and breathed deeply, closing his eyes. Then he brought up the thermal layer. Its expansive dimensions startled the group. "The beings took form using the very land itself, attacking and destroying as they moved. Wherever they were two things happened: the land became extremely cold and their presence blocked my radar. Also, huge thunderstorms appeared right above them. I had used the *Haley's* radar during Trot and David's wedding to look into the massive storms – everything was blocked. Glinda and Ozma were planning on asking for our assistance, and those things struck first. From what we were told later, three villages were overwhelmed and Tina—that little girl—was the only one rescued from the Third Village; she had been forcibly escorted by birds and animals to a safer place just prior to the devastation.

"We had just had all of the personal items and removable gear taken off the *Haley* – including the Plan One Acknowledge Kit. Allen and his crew were charging the secondary batteries for use at the Emerald City. DOC was just walking around. I was inside, and Betsy had arrived earlier to be with Allen. I had been at the radar station..."

He gritted his teeth to prevent tears, but several escaped.

"Suddenly, everything around the *Haley* had been blocked. I went outside and told Allen, who informed me that there had been a tremendous noise way out. It was growing cold. I told Allen to make sure DOC was nearby and I went back up as Betsy was coming down the automated gangplank. She joined me shortly after the fog appeared. That was when they took form and attacked us. They must have gotten DOC first. Betsy and I heard an inhuman scream and felt a thump – one of them must have tried to force its way through the *Haley's* bottom hull. Next thing I knew, Betsy was screaming and this clay-type tentacle crept inside. I grabbed one of the few things left—a long screwdriver—and I stabbed and cut through it. The tentacle pulled back out but what was left behind disintegrated into dust.

I saw Allen, Emilio, and Hector hitting one with their gear, but Allen had been mortally wounded and he went up the gangplank. I begged him to join me inside, but he said it was too late. We both thought about the Geco—the flare gun—and it worked on those creatures! It hurt them. Allen was breathing his last, but I gave him the Geco and the rest of the star shells. I saw Emilio and Hector finally go down and Allen started closing the hull doors."

Composed, Johnathan soldiered on describing those last moments. "Allen knew he was dying, so he must have laid himself on the junction box to let the full current flow from the *Haley's* massive fuel cells into the battery array. The alarms on the *Haley* rang, I held Betsy, and then - b*am!* The array exploded and briefly, everything went dark and then the lights came back on."

"Betsy and I were left alone on the *Haley* all that night with no way to get out. After checking everything and finding some things that had been left behind like blankets, we settled in. However just before that, I had set up the radio to transmit that ping6 command and to route the power for the transmitter via the fuel cells. So, we waited and eventually fell asleep."

"Could you have ever imagined that it was your ping6 signal that eventually led to the *Haley's* discovery around Ceres?" Arial inquired.

"No," he answered. "Now don't ask me how I knew, but I had been told that the Haley would be returned - I just couldn't imagine that was the way it would be found." Fortunately, no one urged him to delve further into his explanation.

"Trot and David had been back at the Emerald City and had been calling in radio updates when we were attacked. Both our radios had been blocked in addition to the radar. That was when they heard the explosion and saw the ball of flames. Finally, they were apprised of what had been going on, and Trot later told me that David had unloaded on Glinda for not briefing him – or using us as an asset.

"My ping6 must have finally gotten through. I remember seeing three of those things and two had been destroyed by the blast, so the effect they had on my technology faded. The last one must have been thrown by the shockwave. That would make sense," he paused and drank, "because once we were rescued by David, Trot, Glinda, and her elite Finest Forty, we were told by someone from the city that the creature had been dragged inside."

Jonathan could tell that they were incredulous at his last statement. "I know what y'all are probably thinking and yes, it became a flustercluck. That thing unleashed outright chaos and it took our Tavors and Lady Glinda doubly enchanting a spear to destroy just one – after it had terribly wounded every single one of the Finest Forty and killed three people in front of Ozma."

"I'd say it was more like it had been setting a trap – good thing for you, David, and the Tavors," Abana stated. "We can provide you about 1000 extra rounds."

"Much obliged, Abana," Jonathan replied.

He continued to describe how the first Bravo mission had been used to determine the track of the creatures – from heading directly to the Emerald City to right towards the Bravo. He explained how Ozma and Dorothy had worked together to destroy the evil and he showed the "before" picture of the Swath of Restoration acquired from the orbital mapping mission. Johnathan played a video of him using a probe from a Geiger counter to demonstrate just how deadly the desert sands were. He talked about how he had first asked permission to marry Betsy and then how he'd proposed to her in front of an entire Throne Room, which elicited a mix of aww's and raspberries! Back and forth they talked until finally, he left off with the orbital mapping mission. As Johnathan stopped, he noticed something: Blith was teary, whispering to her fellow crewmates. She stood up with a hand to her mouth and one by one, the rest followed her.

Johnathan was confused by the quiet tears – until Blith came closer and so did everyone else. She kissed his cheek, placed a finger to his lips, and revealed her heart. "*Yehonatan*," she began, "these tears are both for joy and sadness. You see, this is the last time we will all be together as the same crew – the very one you and the rest mentored. When Abana, Arial, and Amalie were part of the crew that recovered the *Haley*, we still didn't know what had happened." She glanced around. "And had anyone else *but* you had told us, we would have laughed it off as a tall tale."

He chuckled at her words.

"Closure!" she proclaimed and those around her softly said the same.

Johnathan was humbled by her words and had to sit down. As he did, Blith cupped his cheeks. Her words shook him. "We now know. Dear *Yehonatan*, now, we know."

And now I know why I was brought here, He pondered in his heart.

Magnificent Desolation

"You're quite the hopeless romantic, Jonathan," Brian said as he drove the lunar truck to Base Station Five. "Using the Hebrew for 'I love you, Betsy' as the voice password on the 3-D terminal."

Jonathan chuckled. "Guilty as charged, Brian."

"It's cool, man. It's just neat that you've gotten a family back."

"I have to sometimes pinch myself."

"I mean, a gorgeous Princess as a wife and then two cute little girls and an elite soldier as the oldest daughter – and as your second-in-command."

"Yeah, they sure are a gift."

"Of course children are." Brian then got serious. "Do you miss all of this technology from your world?"

"Somewhat, Brian, but it's no longer my home. And from what Earth water can do to me, it's become deadly.

I can never go back."

Brian grunted his acknowledgement and remained silent – they had about 20 minutes left at the truck's normal speed to arrive at their location. He paid attention to the lunar truck's course as it traversed the road designed to minimize the abrasive lunar dust's affect on the various radio receiver arrays.

"Isn't that something else!" He pointed out the lunarscape. "The floor here is dark," he eagerly explained. "That's pretty distinct from the other craters here – more like that found on the near side."

"Yes, I remember that from the Academy training." Jonathan replied. "And during our trips to the moon."

"Now you can see the Central Peaks," he described. "The tallest is over 3200 meters tall."

"Did you ever get a chance to climb it?"

"No, though there are plans for a space-tourism facility in the next five or so years. We did get a flyby once we were here," Brian stated. "I agree that it would be a great workout and an adrenaline rush to accomplish!"

"And some pretty hefty bragging rights!" Jonathan quipped.

"Yep," Brian concurred. "Since I've been here, we have had a chance to explore some of the major features, but with only two people at a time under major communications links and supervision. I'm talking about the volcanic vents, domes, lava tubes, compression ridges, and whatnot. And don't even think about trying to climb those high terraced inner walls – direct orders from my bosses and the ISAs."

Brian smiled at Jonathan's chuckling. "Yeah, some things just aren't worth trying. It's bad enough to be banned from lunar and space service at the least, and at the worst you end up an example in a safety briefing."

"Yes, not very forgiving out here," Jonathan agreed, "but it truly is a magnificent desolation. I never got used to it and it's still amazing. I see the Israeli's used the best of everything for this truck!" he added.

Brian nodded. "The ISA did take most of the ideas from NASA's Space Exploration Vehicle. The cab and compartment sit in the exact center of the chassis. There's enough life support for up to two weeks and there's shielding to enable us to make it to any of the temporary shelters in case of a major solar storm. A crane on top with the portable shelter will be deployed once we get to Base Station Five. The crane has 360-degree movement and a series of cameras that tie in to my own helmet display. Outside, there's a fore and aft driving station with a tool compartment for each - including a winch. There's 12 wheels that can pivot 360 degrees as well." Brian laughed at his last statement. "You should see this thing drive sideways! The tires themselves are the latest airless models, utilizing the nickel titanium shape memory alloy. In fact, they're manufactured at Base Netanyahu. You could drive on the Earth with them." Then he spoke almost in a whisper. "Come to think of it, the raw material for the tires gets sent back to Earth for use in the IDF's own drone vehicles."

"Would we have to go off road to get to the shelters?" Jonathan inquired.

"No, each highway has one that was placed—very, very carefully to not stir up the dust—about mid-way to each base station. We just pivot the wheels and drive in sideways."

"Clever."

"Easy too," Brian asserted. "We've got about another five minutes to get there. So, what did you think of the chemical analysis of the dirt that was found inside the *Haley*?"

"I can see why it was classified Top Secret!" Jonathan affirmed. "No known terrestrial origin! I'd definitely give the thumbs up for that."

"I thought it was funny when Abana and Amalie had all but carried Arial up to us, saying *'speaking of love...'*" Brian teased and they both laughed.

"That was, Brian," Jonathan replied. "Kyle DeLeon was a neat guy. I'm sad that he passed away, but I'm thrilled he and Arial found each other. I appreciate the folks back in Charleston made the monument to the *Haley*, Kyle's grave and memorial right next to it."

"About a minute to go," Brian announced. "Think they'll do something about the Bravo even though the *Haley* is basically a memorial on the moon – located at Base Sumter?"

"With everything wiped and the electronics a total loss, yeah, I can see them bringing it back to the Southern Republic," Johnathan answered. "Maybe even make it a memorial of sorts right next to the one for the *Haley* and Kyle. One could even imagine the *Golda Meir* being the one to bring it back as a sign of good faith."

"I can see that too," Brian agreed. "Okay, we're here. Now, watch this!" He stopped the truck and then activated the crane, swinging and extending it. "See what I'm seeing?" he asked as he shared the video against a window on Jonathan's side. "This is right from the camera's view on the crane." He waited for Jonathan's 'yes' and then continued. "We're now right above the instrumentation module." He pressed a button. "Now what's happening is inert gas—nitrogen—is being pumped into the inflatable walls of the shelter. They're made from the same material as the expandable space habitation modules," he explained as the walls started to inflate downwards until they came in contact with the surface around the instrumentation module. "I'm now using the crane to apply some pressure from the top to ensure a good seal."

"What's that?" Jonathan asked, pointing outside at something expanding into view.

"A portable passageway," Brian disclosed. "It'll travel in sections until it reaches the shelter, where it will connect itself with extreme precision. It's still a vacuum, but it prevents any lunar dust from getting into the module as we work. Got the spare routing module and terminal?" Jonathan lifted both up. "Let's check our suites before we egress."

That being done, Brian typed a quick message on the truck's console terminal and sent it, only leaving when he received a response from Abner. He grabbed two cases: one with tools and the other containing a type of dust remover.

"Let's go." He had the oxygen evacuated from the truck cab before Jonathan unlatched the side door. He led the way down the narrow passageway with his helmet lights glaring. It was quiet and uneventful except for status messages being displayed on his helmet visor – made of aluminum oxynitride, which gave it unbelievable hardness. There was no bunny-hopping for this, just simple, slow walking. Arriving at the entrance of the shelter, Brian unzipped the outer door and then the inner and walked in.

"Go ahead and zip those back up," he said once Jonathan was inside as well.

"Rather cramped here," Jonathan commented.

"Just enough for two people. You're a lot bigger than Abner so there's not as much space left over!" Brian joked.

"Ha ha!" Jonathan shot back sarcastically.

"Here," Brian said, "take this powered screwdriver and unlatch the outer panel labeled 'Routing'."

Jonathan did as he was told, taking a knee in the suit to do so. "That's pretty comfortable," he remarked as he performed the operation.

"Yes, the pads are made from a special kind of memory foam," Brian answered. "Now that we've got that panel off, remove the next one and the one behind it." As Jonathan did so, Brian placed the screws into a small container and laid each panel against the instrumentation panel – far enough from their feet so they wouldn't kick it over.

"The final panel needs to be removed and that is the one that contains the routing module," Brian instructed, watching as Jonathan completed the task. "Remove the module by pushing down the center button on the handle." And he took it from him. "Insert the new module all the way in and then try to gently remove it. Very good, Jonathan," he complimented. "It's my turn now, so please hand me the terminal."

The terminal was nothing more than an extremely radiation-hardened and environmentally protected tablet. The screen itself was made from the same type of material as Brian's helmet visor. The icons were purposely bigger than normal, and Brian used a stylus to copy and paste in the configuration.

"I see this module was made in 2028," Jonathan said.

"Yeah, it's the oldest module and you're the oldest guy, so that's why we needed your help."

"Aren't you the comedian."

"Got to have a good sense of humor."

"Oh boy!" Brian suddenly exclaimed and gulped hard enough that Jonathan heard it over their miniature communications network.

"An oops?" Jonathan asked.

"Perhaps," Brian quickly replied and tapped the terminal some more. "We might have a problem. I'm not getting any routes." He continued tapping away.

Jonathan's response was a slow-building, hearty laugh. "Hey, genius!" he announced with enormous sarcasm.

"Yeah?" A frustrated, Brian responded.

"Did you forget 'no shut'?" he teased in a child-like voice.

There was a pause as Brian typed in the commands to show the configuration. "Um...oops."

"Not bad for the 'old guy', eh?"

"Routes came up!" Brian declared.

"Mm-hmm."

"Okay," Brian said, chortling, "you got me, old man."

Both laughed hard for several minutes. "Routes still good?" Jonathan quizzed.

"Sure are!" Brian answered. "Let's wrap everything up. But before you put each panel back on, let me use this to ensure no dust is left behind." He removed a small hose and nozzle from one container.

"Lead the way, young buck!" Jonathan quipped.

"Decades before centuries!" Brian hurled right back.

After about 25 minutes, everything was completed and the shelter deflated; the passageway returned to the side of the truck. Brian refilled the cab with oxygen and lifted his visor. He kept his gloves on until Jonathan raised his own visor, using a finger to smudge his cheek with lunar dust.

"Hey! That stuff is abrasive!" Jonathan complained. "Where did that come from anyway?"

"While you were walking back, I dabbed a little from a small box made just for this occasion," he explained.

"What do you mean?" he protested as Brian smudged the other cheek!

"Welcome to the Systems Engineers," Brian proudly informed him, giving Johnathan a shoulder slap and a firm handshake. "You've done real work; now you get to show it! Congrats!"

"Oh," Jonathan said. "That's real cool, Brian." They gave each other a fist-bump.

Thank you, Brother

Ozma took a sip of the fizzy, grapefruit flavored water as she overlooked the Garden. It had been a very, very productive day and at the end, a chance flick of mud ended up being an all-out mud war between her and Chatulah. Both of her cheeks were dirty – as was the rest of her jumpsuit. "The shower can't come soon enough," she whispered with a smile.

She waved at her roommate, who was collecting some fruit in the distance. Seeing the happy reply, Ozma pulled up her legs and sighed deeply. "I want to go home," she said on a sigh. *Please, I want to go home. Oh Dorothy, I miss you so much,* her heart cried out, and this time there was no answer. She pulled her legs close and just sat, holding back the tears.

"Hey there, stranger!" a voice yelled and it was Jonathan at the base of the platform. "Mind if I join you?"

"Please, do!" Ozma answered with a grin. She observed as he backed up, took a running start, and leaped upwards towards the platform. He landed gracefully next to her. "You made it look easy!" She quipped. "The first time I tried, I crashed on top of Chatulah!"

"That had to be interesting to see!" Jonathan joked. "It does take some getting used to. Looks like we've both been kept busy here." He gestured to her soiled jumpsuit.

"Yes. Chatulah really needed help in the Garden."

"I've heard through the grapevine that she really appreciates what you've been able to do with her."

Ozma grabbed his hand. "That is very kind of you to say." She didn't let go as they both became quiet and looked over the Garden together.

"Your people have accomplished an amazing feat here, Jonathan," Ozma finally declared, pointing towards the Garden. "Of all locations to have a place like this... underground – and on the moon!" She observed him nodding as he took a sip from his own bottle, quietly belching.

Ozma giggled. "Is yours grapefruit flavored?"

"No, but it's one of the diet soda ones. Which reminds me, with all the goodies we have in addition to the new Bravo, we'll be getting one of those on-demand soda machines and multiple flavors – including grapefruit."

She became thoughtful and her voice nearly cracked. "Are you happy to be back in your world?"

He took a long swig and stared out over the Garden. "You know, this place here is more than just for food. The *Haley* had done a couple trips to Mars before we arrived in Oz. You have to imagine being surrounded by technology for days on end – 90 sometimes. The air is recycled, the food is good, but..." He paused. "You rely on hoping and praying everything is working as it should.

Relying on your shipmates because outside the ship is an environment that will kill you. A rest stop like this Garden would have been a Godsend. It would have been a touch of home. The effect on morale would be immeasurable."

Does he want to stay? She squeezed his hand.

He turned and faced her, sitting crossed-legged. "But this place, it's not home, Ozma. My world, yes, but my home is with Betsy, Anusha, Tina, Tara, David, Trot, and...you." His eyes met hers.

Oh Jonathan. Thank you, brother! Finally, some tears started to flow down her cheeks.

"Hey, hey," he said softly, cupping her cheeks.

"I'm sorry they're filthy," she confessed with a weak smile. He in turn showed her the lunar dust on his own face. "A badge of honor," he explained. "Brian smudged my cheeks and welcomed me into the Systems Engineers after having done real work here." He chuckled and Ozma smiled back.

She blushed as he caressed her skin as she cried. "You miss her, don't you?" he asked and she just shook her head in agreement. "You *and* I will be going back. We have to have faith," he declared with a soothing look in his eyes that warmed Ozma's heart. "We will be back, and we'll be with the ones we love – especially you with Dorothy."

She hugged him tightly for that, mud and all. With their heads close to each other and their eyes shut. Neither saw the faint glow emanating from their foreheads.

After a few minutes, they released the embrace and turned once more out towards the Garden. She felt a gentle poke. "Oh, I want to thank you for healing my arm," he expressed. "We both know how little I accept that."

She beamed at his grateful words. "You are most welcome. How is it?"

"Much better, obviously," he admitted. "A scratching

sensation every so often—kind of like a rash—but it's doing quite well."

She was delighted at this. "I take it this won't be talked about once we're back?" she asked with a mischievous gleam in her eye.

"See? You *know* we'll be back!" He chuckled and she placed a hand to her mouth and softly laughed. "And I now understand why *I* was brought here – closure for the *Golda Meir* crew. They never really knew what happened."

"Jonathan?" She asked, becoming quite serious.

"Yes, Ozma?"

"Have you..." She paused.

"Is something wrong?" He inquired with concern.

"No," she replied. "Have you ever heard of the Romani?"

"Oh yes, I sure have," He answered. "Another group that suffered tremendously during the Holocaust."

"I know," Ozma acknowledged. "I have learned much from Chatulah – her great-grandmother was Romani and survived Auschwitz."

"One of the lucky few," Jonathan concurred. "The Romani have been persecuted for a very long time, too."

"That is sad. I feel for them," Ozma professed.

"And just like any other group, they have had their fair share of derogatory names."

"They have?"

"Oh yes, but I'd rather not say. It's just not polite or right."

She touched his arm. "You can tell me."

"I'm not certain how Chatulah would take to you using that term, Ozma," he protested.

"You know I won't take offense."

He looked at her and back at the Garden. "Chatulah is walking towards us."

"Please?" she begged, wishing to know. "I won't repeat it to her."

"Okay, okay," he acquiesced and leaned in closer, whispering, "Gypsies."

Ozma didn't answer, tilting her head.

"Well, your roomie is here." He declared once Chatulah had arrived at the platform. "I need to get cleaned up anyway." Johnathan stood and jumped off the edge, landing about five meters away.

"Ozma?" Chatulah requested.

"Yes?"

"How would you like to join me and the rest on the CIC? It looks like Amalie from the *Golda Meir* figured out how you and *Yehonatan* made your presence known so you could be rescued!" She was excited.

"I would love to!" Ozma replied and quickly jumped off the platform.

As she walked behind Chatulah, a thought came to her like a rushing wind: *Gypsies...where have I heard that before?*

From...Oz?!

With the exception of Aitan, Abra, and the twins, the CIC was basically empty this late in the evening. Two smart boards had hand-written drawings and notes on them. Chatulah softly chuckled at the scene of Ashu and Asher trying to explain things to Ozma. The lanky twins towered over her, but it was Ozma who intimidated them. They were awkward, but informative as she listened to their discussions. It was mostly one-way with Ozma nodding as they spoke.

"Ozma has been a great help, hasn't she?" Aitan asked once he walked up to her and Chatulah nodded in agreement.

"A little rough in the beginning, but we've managed a miracle: we won't have any loss despite the greater than normal growth," Chatulah declared. "The remaining work can be handled by me now. It's...it's been a pleasure, actually," she also quietly admitted. "She was an eager learner and an even more enthusiastic helper."

"This has been a most interesting time for all of us, Chatulah," Aitan stated.

"How much longer?"

She heard Aitan sigh before he rubbed his chin. "We don't know. We simply don't know. After the briefing that *Yehonatan* gave earlier, we believe the reason *he's* here was that the *Golda Meir* crew got closure. His shipmates were their original mentors. They now know everything that happened."

"Which then leaves just Ozma," Chatulah pondered out loud. "Why is she here?"

"Leave that one for the rabbis, Chatulah!" he quipped. "Laila Tov." (Good Night.) He patted her shoulder before he walked away.

Chatulah crossed her arms and continued to observe the three. *She's handling herself quite well around them,* she thought. Yehonatan *must have shown her that.* She smiled.

Slowly, she read off the first smart board that had a circle with the words "Planet Oz" written on it. A smaller circle was labeled "wormhole". She overheard the twins explaining how they had grabbed several cables to help visualize the radio signals and these they had placed between the two smart boards. She grinned as Ashu hopped like a bunny to act out and explain how they traversed the wormhole.

Chatulah then looked at the other smart board that had the smaller circle, again labeled "wormhole" and a crude drawing of the moon. She started to hear a strange whistling coming from the CIC's speakers and deduced one of the twins must have started playing the sound.

She had slowly returned to looking at the one with the moon when she nearly gave herself whiplash looking back at the first smart board.

Her hand went up to her mouth and she felt weak as her eyes locked onto a single word: Oz!

Chatulah's heart nearly stopped. *Oz? That little girl in the picture has that on her forehead. I wonder if Ozma might know that little girl. I need to show her great-grandmother's picture!*

10ᵀᴴ OF ADAR, 5805
(MONDAY, 27 FEBRUARY 2045)

Ozma wept bitter tears from the farthest reaches of her soul as she floated above the desert of human ash and the mountains of countless personal items. The hot wind whipped her dress and hair and seared her lungs as she struggled to breathe. In her hand was the source of her grief: a tiny bone.

The bone itself pierced through to the very fabric of her being. She knew, just who its owner had been...

From afar, Ozma had watched the two sisters play peek-a-boo with each other as the packed rail car continued its journey. She could tell they truly loved one another – the older was a girl of 16 or maybe 17 while the youngest was perhaps 3. Ozma smiled at the thought of them being an island of love inside the train car of woe. Every time the older sister looked up, Ozma had to turn away for fear of being impolite.

Finally, the train came to a stop, the car doors were unlatched, and everyone was rushed out via harsh words in an unknown language, the barks of dogs, and men with guns. Accustomed to the darkness of the rail car, Ozma had to cover her eyes with her dirty hands to shield herself from the bright sun of clear yet mild day.

Ozma saw an impeccably-dressed man atop a platform overseeing the whole operation as the crowds disembarked and finally were gathered. Waving his right hand as if he were simply shooing away a fly, the two sisters were forcibly separated. The older went right while the younger cried hysterically, tiny hands reaching out for a sister who could no longer be with her.

The little girl was held by an older woman and the group of eight began to march, as did she, with the rest towards a path. And as they walked, from the very front and working its way backward, a song of despair departed from each throat – man, woman; young and old. It mattered not. It was as if they all knew.

And so did Ozma.

Arriving at a building, it didn't shock anyone when they were told to disrobe prior to having a "shower". They entered the building the same way they had arrived: with their death-song. Ozma stood near a wall, deep scratches gouged in it with the remains of many nails. She did not wait long; once the last person had entered and the doors were bolted shut, the gas came in and the crowd panicked. It was the young who passed the quickest, and Ozma witnessed the child die before her own life was snubbed out – crushed by the throngs who had tried to climb the walls in vain.

In her spirit form, she watched as the room was emptied of bodies. Outside, the guards casually picked through the clothes of the dead. They were laughing – it had all been a day on the job. She floated along near the child's body until it had been placed into a nearby oven without a second glance.

Tear after tear flowed down Ozma's cheeks as she tenderly cupped the tiny bone. It had been part of the hand that had held out for her big sister. All became quiet and still. In her heart, Ozma knew what was coming.

"Ask for her forgiveness," the still small voice directed.

Ozma's mouth was dry as she struggled to respond.

"Ask for her forgiveness," the still small voice repeated.

She looked far up towards a sky that seemed cold and indifferent to her plight. But then, off in the far, far distance, she could see a light. Glancing upon it, she finally found the courage to speak. "Please. Please show me."

Ozma suddenly recalled the scene of the two sisters being separated and she peered deep into the eyes of the older sister. In seconds, something Chatulah had told her etched itself upon her heart:

I have her very eyes!

She awoke. The room was dark, but she sensed her roommate moving around. Turning her head, she confirmed her suspicions. Chatulah stood by her great-grandmother's picture with a piece of paper in her hand. She didn't say anything, but she glanced up at the ceiling and quietly sighed.

A path to take

Chatulah walked along paths covered by a yellow-white pollen. Upon glancing up at the tremendous hill in the background, she knew immediately where she was and smiled: Kibbutz Sassa! The air was sweetened by apple blossoms, the wind gentle upon her face. The weather was comfortable in her khaki shorts, tank top, and sandals. It felt good to be dreaming of her beloved kibbutz.

She breathed it all in, this magical place. The birds happily chirped away and she could hear the day-to-day operations of the kibbutz. Thus, she walked until she nearly tripped over a rock and noticed a fork in the path – a scroll-shaped candy was at the entrance to each.

Confused, all sound disappeared and only her heartbeat and exhalations could be heard. The candies were quite different in color and aroma as Chatulah examined each one. The piece near the path going left had a sweet, honey smell. Its colors were like that of different types of ice cream – such as orange or chocolate. Intrigued, she ate this one first.

The candy dissolved rapidly in her mouth. It was almost too sweet as it trickled down her throat.

Chatulah's grin became a scowl as her stomach soured. Her body began to ache, and she fell to the ground clutching her chest. "Am I having a heart attack?" she gasped out loud. "Help!" she yelled, but no one came. Then, the hand around her heart began to throb in pain and she looked at it in horror – it was frozen! Her heart had frozen solid. It had the color of solid blue ice and her hand displayed the ravages of severe frostbite.

Blinking, she was standing again at the fork in the path. Somehow, Chatulah knew she had to try the candy on the right. It was plain, with none of the flashy colors or sweet scent of its counterpart. However, there was a fragrance to it—like fresh apple blossoms—as she lifted it up to her nose. Sighing with trepidation, she ate the candy.

It was a harsh taste – much like a cough drop made from licorice. Surprisingly, she could eventually taste the fragrance with every chew. Swallowing, she waited with bated breath. An eruption of heartache gripped her and she wept. The tears hit the ground and released little puffs of pollen. It went on for an unknown amount of time. Such heartbreak the manner she had never encountered before. "The pain!" she cried out and fell to her knees.

Then slowly, strange emotions began to enter her heart: relief and then...freedom from the pain. And it was not freedom from physical pain, but a long-held burden being removed. She took deep breaths and each one strengthened the feeling.

Chatulah blinked and again saw herself at the fork in the path with the two candies. She pondered the meaning of it all.

She awoke and remembered every detail of her dream. Climbing out of bed, she walked over to the picture of her great-grandmother and removed the paper of the One behind it. There she stood, gazing at the figure, her fingers skimming along the "OZ" written on the young girl's forehead.

Hearing Ozma's movements behind her, she put the picture away and remained standing before going back to bed. Sleep evaded her; all she could do was stare at the ceiling.

Party in the Mess

In contrast to Ozma and Chatulah, the Mess was anything but gloomy. It was somewhat crowded, but cozy. Aitan had his crew present—as did Abana—and between Blith's music and Lenah's singing, everyone was having a grand time.

Aitan smiled at Ashu and Asher as they made the best of the crowded room and impromptu festivities. "Don't forget, *Yehonatan*," he overheard Asher call out, "we gave you six of our favorite controllers and that console has more emulators and ROMs than you can imagine." Aitan watched as *Yehonatan* gave the thumbs up.

Aitan turned to Abana—who had stayed by his side—and commented, "That gifting had to have been hard for Ashu and Asher. They like their games, and this little 'party' is hard on them."

"I can imagine they have their moments despite their autism?" Abana responded.

"Yes, especially when it comes to my family's hummus – I have to be on watch for their swiping. They got me pretty good yesterday!" he quipped. "But they're the best comms techs I have ever seen or known."

Abana nodded as both continued to listen in and observe the group. Lenah described how some freshly-made Hamantaschen had been vacuumed-sealed as a gift when something struck Aitan. He called for everyone to pause their fun, which resulted in the well-known boos and stomping of feet during Purim celebrations.

"Does anybody know where Chatulah and Ozma are?" he asked.

"They came in about an hour ago," Judah replied. "They both looked tired and only grabbed some pastries and tea."

"Should they be here?" Aitan joked to everyone.

"Yes!" was the rowdy response.

"Lenah, please go get those two. It's bad enough I've

got one human cat, and it seems she's influenced another." he requested, and Lenah happily bounded off.

"Now, resume the –"He began to say, but the party resumed on its own.

The Awful Revelation

Ozma took another sip of her tea as she sat on Chatulah's bed. They had eaten their pastries rather quickly upon returning to the room and the soft music that played did its best to sooth them. Both were exhausted, and Ozma yawned again when she observed Chatulah—who stood with her back to her—do the same. *Should now be the time I ask her about the gypsies?* she pondered.

It took some time for her to build up enough courage. "Chatulah?" But her roommate had pulled out the paper from behind the picture and faced her.

"Ozma," Chatulah said, "let's go back to the garden. The date palms have some old fronds that need to be pruned. I left some tools beside them before I met back up with you. It should be an easy job and we can take a nap afterward."

Ozma nodded but sensed that Chatulah wasn't done.

"I know you are from Oz," she confessed. "This paper I am holding is a picture of the One who sent my great-grandmother's people away. She drew it over 110 years ago."

"That was a terrible thing to do to them." Ozma stated.

"I know," Chatulah answered with a sigh. "It's of a young girl. You might know her so if I let you look at it, could you pass on a message from me?"

A young girl? Ozma's heart questioned. *I don't allow that many to practice magic in my kingdom - especially back then. Was this a witch? I must consult with Glinda when I get back.*

"I will gladly do so," Ozma replied with a cheerful smile.

Beaming at her words, Chatulah handed Ozma the paper and resumed facing away from her, taking a sip from her mug.

Ozma set her own cup on the floor and studied the yellowish paper that betrayed its great age. It felt fragile and the smell of old books clung to it. She started to carefully, deliberately unfold the paper until it was all laid out. Ozma's eyes fell upon the young girl in the picture, and she stared straight back at her. The terrifying image caused her heart to stop and she stared straight ahead, immediately falling into a waking dream...

She was running down the hallways of her Royal Palace. Behind her, numerous figures gave chase. No one recognized her adult appearance. She had to stop Ozma! She just had to!

"I know I can make her stop," she told herself after she rounded the final corner. Pushing the young woman who stood at the main door aside, she ran into the room. "I know where she is. Stop, Ozma!" she yelled at the top of her voice. "Stop!"

She was about to enter the room where the younger Ozma had just taken out the Magic Belt. Abruptly, she was flung back by some kind of invisible wall, only to be smirked at by the One. Quickly, she got to her feet and tried to force her way inside. This time, her shoulders erupted in pain; the invisible wall was immovable. Time was running out – she could her the others gathering outside. "No, Ozma!" She pounded against the wall.

The One clasped the Magic Belt. At this, Ozma began to scream even louder, large tears cascading down her cheeks. "No! Please no! Don't – they can stay in Oz! Let them stay, Ozma!"

The One placed her hands on her hips. Frantically, older-Ozma smacked the wall harder. "Ozma! No! No! No!" There wasn't a response, so she yelled as loud as she could. "Don't! Stop! No! No! No!"

Then, the One simply waved her hands and the deed was executed. Ozma collapsed to the floor and wept. "Why? They did nothing to you!" She grieved. "Nothing!"

The One simply smiled and started walking away.

Then in a menacing way, began to creep towards her. She tried to scoot away, but then Ozma felt many hands holding her down as she struggled to break free. The One seemed to shimmer as she crawled through the invisible wall.

Ozma was kicking her feet as much as possible, but still, the One kept slithering towards her. The first hand grasped her feet and she became numb all over; her limbs became cold. The One came closer and closer, and those holding her seemed to be laughing at her expense.

Onward the One crept until she was right above her face. The One dug her nails into Ozma's shoulders and then began merging with her! It was the most agonizing experience Ozma had ever experienced. The cells in her chest burned and her heart raced. The merging continued and Ozma could hear two heartbeats. And then, there was only one: hers and hers alone.

From the deepest part of her soul, a massive geyser of woe pushed itself upward and outward. With great heartache, Ozma knew that the One who sent Chatulah's people away was her. There was no evil enchantment that had caused her actions – no outside force chilled her heart. She had done it all of her own free will. The One and her were one and the same!

Her shrieks of recognition shattered the waking dream and caused a loud crash – a surprised Chatulah dropping her mug on the floor. Still holding the picture, Ozma sprinted out of the room, barely hearing the thump of the door as she hit someone. Onward she ran towards the only sanctuary she knew here: the Garden. From behind her, Ozma could hear Chatulah.

The Mess

The dancing had just begun when Aitan glimpsed Lenah dashing to the mess. She was rubbing her nose and her face displayed great concern. Aitan motioned for the festivities to die down.

"What's wrong, Lenah?" he quizzed. "Did they refuse to join us?" He was somewhat hurt upon seeing her return alone.

"No!" Lenah got out. "Something terrible must have happened," she explained. "I heard Ozma scream just before I neared the door and the next thing I knew, it flew open before I had a chance to block it. I saw Ozma shot out with a piece of paper and Chatulah chased after her."

Everyone's faces became worried. "Where were they heading?"

"I'm guessing the Garden," Lenah answered.

Aitan looked around at the group. "I may need some help," he announced while glancing at Abana. "Let's go before something worse happens."

All followed after him as he bolted from the area.

The Truth Revealed

Chatulah began to close the gap between her and Ozma. *Was that a relative?* she pondered. *Was it someone she knew really well?* They entered the Garden, only separated by five meters of distance. "Ozma, stop!" Chatulah yelled.

Ozma kept running, weeping and ignoring her.

They were nearing the palm trees when Chatulah noticed Ozma had dropped the picture. "I'll use my knowledge of the moon's gravity," she said under her breath and leaped, flying over Ozma and landing just in front of her. The two collided against one of the palm trees.

Chatulah stood as Ozma scooted up to a tree – she was crying hysterically. Chatulah bent to one knee to try to talk to her, but she was pushed away. Out of the corner of her eye, she saw Aitan approaching with a group of people about ten meters away.

"Ozma, was that young girl a relative?" she asked in a firm, booming voice. All Ozma did was shake her head. "Was she a close friend?" Chatulah stood over her.

"No!" Ozma finally screamed so loud it took Chatulah by surprise and she backed off a bit. Ozma stood with her back against the palm tree. She turned towards the group first and then back to Chatulah, whose eyes locked with hers.

"Chatulah," Ozma lamented aloud, "I am the One!"

"What?" gasped Chatulah, shocked.

"I am the One who sent the Gypsies away!"

With bated breath

Aitan and the rest watched the unbelievable scene unfold. Someone had picked up the picture and one by one, they had passed it around. Chatulah had only confided to him that she possessed such a picture – drawn by her great-grandmother. Abana handed it to Aitan and he intently studied its details. "It's just a picture drawn by a young girl," he commented softly.

But! his heart thought and he looked for someone who could help. Finding him, he called, *"Yehonatan!"*

Once Johnathan was at the front of the group, Aitan gave him the picture.

Everyone else must have had the same idea, Aitan speculated, since the others were also observing Jonathan's reaction. Once Jonathan had had time to really examine the picture, Aitan watched his eyes grow wide. "Oh, my goodness," he heard him say. "That *is* Ozma – when she was a young princess!"

Aitan gasped with the rest. "Then the stories were true," he deduced.

Suddenly, Abana grabbed his arm and pointed with her free hand. There, with a garden tool held high, Chatulah was threatening Ozma. "Oh no, don't do it, Chatulah!" he pleaded out loud. They all moved in closer in case they had to intervene – and carefully watched and waited.

Chatulah's Painful Choice

Great-grandmother, the One! Chatulah's heart cried. She held the tree pruner aloft, ready to cut down and at long last avenge.

Ozma had collapsed to the ground. Chatulah saw her defenseless state and paused. "How could you?" she declared, about to strike. Her heart pounded in her ears and adrenaline surged through her blood. She could taste the revenge. "You sent them back – not once thinking what that might mean," she thundered.

"I didn't know. I didn't know," Ozma repeated in horror. "I never –"

"Never checked up on them?" Chatulah cut her off. "You, with the device that allows you to see everything, anywhere; even on Earth?" Tears started to flow from her broken heart and hurt soul.

"No, I never checked up on them. I didn't check up on others that had been sent away either," Ozma confessed.

Chatulah's chest burned with rage. The words from her great-grandmother were streaming from their memories, taking control of her hands. Her muscles tensed. *Avenge us!* She could hear their words; she could see her great-grandmother once again as she lay dying. *Avenge us!*

Still, Chatulah hesitated, struggling to speak. "I told you!" she declared. "I told you the true stories of what they did – especially to the children!" Ozma only nodded. "The twins! Ozma, you had the nightmare about the twins. The children were used as sick science experiments. How could you, Ozma! Why?"

"I'm sorry. I'm so sorry. I never could have imagined what would have been done to them. I thought evil could be –"

"Evil could be what?" Chatulah demanded, the veins in her arms bulging.

"I thought evil only needed to be made to forget back then. I was wrong. I was so wrong. I was so naive." Ozma wept again.

Chatulah nearly lost control. "You still are Ozma! You, with all that power, sent an entire population to their deaths. You never checked on them. You never even brought them back. My great-grandmother was the only one of nine to survive, Ozma. How could you!" She slammed the tool into the ground, mere inches from her target. She raised it again and noticed that Ozma had seemed to accept her fate. She was all hers.

Ozma's lips quivered, her expression that of a woman in acceptance of the terribly wrong things she had done. "I'm..."

Chatulah barely heard Ozma and she let her have it. "What!"

"I'm not that powerful. I only have simple fairy powers. I'm...I'm..."

Chatulah waited, ready to deliver sweet vengeance.

"I'm not perfect!" Ozma confessed with tears of anguish and pain. "I made a mistake. I was a young princess then. I am so sorry." She cried softly as she looked up into Chatulah's eyes.

Ozma's confession touched Chatulah's heart, but her hands were still shaking. "All these years," she began, tears forming in her eyes, "hearing the stories. What they and their kind did. So, so many willing collaborators." The tears commenced streaming down her skin and her voice cracked. "I swore if I could *ever* avenge them..."

She breathed heavily and snarled. "Here, right in front of me..." Ozma's eyes displayed pure dread and with a loud war cry, she swung the tool down with all she had.

And purposely missed Ozma – who was hugging her knees to her chest!

The impact created a small cloud of dust that seemed to hang over them. Chatulah also collapsed to the ground, using the pruning tool to support her as she stared at a shaking and whimpering Ozma. Lifting her head upward, Her heart cried out in deep, deep pain and poured forth her lamentations from *Exodus 34: 6-7*.

"waYaávor y'hwäh al-Pänäyw waYiq'rä y'hwäh y'hwäh ël rachûn w'chaNûn erekh' aPayim w'rav-chešed weémet notzër chešed läáläfiym nosë äwon wäfesha w'cha‡ääh w'naQëh lo y'naQeh Poqëd áwon ävôt al-Bäniym w'al-B'nëy väniym al-shiLëshiym w'al-riBëiym"

Chatulah wept bitter tears, hand pounding the ground. Her grief was loud and soon filled the entire Garden. With a scream, she threw the pruning tool far away and her hands grasped at the dirt.

Despite her weeping, she inched closer to Ozma. Ever so closer she edged. Her heart raced with all manner of thoughts as their eyes met and the two women glanced into each other's souls. Chatulah remembered her Tanakh and her heart spoke to her: *She couldn't have known what would happen a few short years later. She's not all powerful. She was a young princess – so very, very naive. She couldn't have known what her actions then would do later.*

She never expected these feelings. They were painful, yet they brought consolation.

"Chatulah," Ozma said softly. "I...I can only ask for your...for your forgiveness."

Forgiveness! The very statement caused both women's eyes to grow wide and an incredible realization struck them. Chatulah and Ozma clasped each other's cheeks.

"For this point in time, and for such a time as this," Chatulah started.

"We were brought together." Ozma finished.

With a great sigh, Chatulah drew Ozma to her and they embraced with tears of relief. "My great-grandmother only knew the younger from a distance, but I have gotten to know the older personally," she quietly conveyed. "That young princess no longer exists. You are not her anymore." Ozma squeezed Chatulah in response. Her tears moistened Chatulah's shoulder and they hugged even tighter. "Ozma..." Chatulah whispered, "Ozma of Oz, I forgive you."

The Whistler

It was late morning – several hours after the incident in the Garden – and all was fairly normal and routine in the CIC. Reclining in their seats at the Center Console, Ashu and Asher watched videos on advanced communications concepts while Abra, Abner, and Brian conducted routine network and systems checks.

"You guys ever get tired of those?" Brian quipped at the Twins' choice of "entertainment". Asher answered him with a loud "No!" Suddenly, an alert message popped onto the mounted displays, the speakers delivering a corresponding notification sound.

Ashu and Asher became all business and paused the training videos. Asher stood while his brother stayed seated.

"NEW DATABASE ENTRY DETECTED!" a display announced.

"It's got to be a Whistler," declared Asher as he and the rest watched the results.

"VLF SIGNAL." Asher gave a victory hoot.

"RECEIVING BASE STATIONS:1...2...3...4...5..."

At this, everyone joined Ashu and Asher in celebrating.

"COMPUTING LOCATION..."

"I bet it's 290 kilometers right above us," Asher predicted and sure enough, the display values proved him right!

"PLAY SIGNAL? (Y/N)"

Asher nodded for his brother to do so. The descending tones gave the Twins reason to clap.

Abra spoke up. "We need to inform Aitan."

"No," Asher stated firmly - which caused Abra and her crew to raise their eyebrows at his bluntness. "We need to inform our aunt first," He explained quite happily.

"Your aunt?" Abner inquired.

"Our Aunt Abana!" the two brothers blurted out as one.

At this, Abra and her crew just laughed. "Okay, you guys have thirty minutes." She informed them.

"Email already sent as you were talking, Abra!" announced Asher with a wide smile - his brother's grin was even bigger as they rubbed their hands with glee.

My Spies

Abana was crouching, hiding behind the Center Console—no easy feat, since she was wearing her spacesuit—and waited for Aitan to arrive. Her nephews were enjoying the fruits of their intelligence gathering: hummus and expensive dates.

Soon enough, she overheard Aitan's confused questioning. "Asher and Ashu, where did you get that?"

Abana stood and laughed. "Moses had his spies," she cheerfully voiced. "And my nephews have been mine. They've always been eager to please, and they are *very* easy to please." Both grinned at her, lifting their bowls up in appreciation.

Aitan laughed with the rest of his crew in the CIC. "They have outwitted me again," he declared to Abana. "I take it you and the *Golda Meir* are ready for launch?"

"Yes, everyone is aboard and standing by. We have some distinguished guests that need to return home. Besides, if Amalie was correct, we'll see the wormhole itself," Abana explained.

"Then me and Chatulah will join you as we send off Ozma and *Yehonatan*. We'll have a quick goodbye with everyone else here."

"Very well," Abana said, leaving the CIC to join her crew.

The Wormhole

Abana and Abira were at the controls as the *Golda Meir* came to a full stop through its maneuvering rockets. From the optical array, they could see the wormhole and enabled enough magnification so it filled the entire cockpit display. They were at a position some-30 kilometers away.

Amalie floated behind them and both her CO and XO reached to shake her hands. *"Kol hakavod!"* (Well done! Bravo!) Abana proudly proclaimed. "This may eventually be a Nobel Prize!"

"I'm just glad to see it," Amalie said with a shrug.

The wormhole was a wonder to behold, like a magnificent two-kilometer wide marble that reflected and diffracted the light every which way. "Who's all for going into that?" Abana quipped.

"I'm certain every one of us is," Amalie retorted, "but it isn't meant for us."

"Leave it for the Rabbis, eh?" Abana inferred.

"Yes," Amalie softly replied.

"Where are our guests anyway?" Abana wished to know.

"*Yehonatan* has already said his goodbyes and is with Blith and Arial in the upper bay with the Bravo," Amalie explained. "Ozma is with Chatulah, Aitan, and the rest of the crew near the Table Display."

Abana smiled at her Chief Engineer in response and resumed observing the wonder before her. "Will you look at that?" she suddenly announced, highlighting the section that had captured her attention. "There!" She pointed.

Near the very center of the wormhole, though somewhat distorted, was an image of a planet. "Just as we would expect, we're seeing the other end," Amalie discussed.

"I'd love to know just how many light-years the distance is," Abana pondered out loud. "Maybe one day..."

They all nodded with her and continued watching for a few extra moments. "Well, it's time," Abana decided. "After Ozma says goodbye, we'll let Chatulah and Aitan watch their entry into the wormhole from up here."

The Bravo

With Blith and Arial overseeing him, Jonathan completed his final checks. "The booster attachment will clear the Bravo of the *Golda Meir* and then propel you to the correct speed. It'll jettison after 20 seconds and its own retrorockets will reverse its course," Blith informed him.

Jonathan nodded. "I see that my readouts are...exactly where my old Bravo left off."

"Technically, the Bravo is running a pseudo-simulation," Arial explained. "We managed to have the flight systems to use the old fuel data and other settings."

"Root has its privileges!" Jonathan quipped and Blith and Arial laughed with him. "Just when will this 'simulation' mode end?" he wanted to know.

"Once you have landed, the real settings will take effect one hour after the Bravo has been sent into systems standby and engine shutdown," Arial answered. "You will notice a little Star of David on the lower right of the screen when accessing the internal system information logs via the web portal. Selecting it will revert the screen to English."

"That will be a shock," Jonathan stated. "What else?"

"We tried very hard, but you will notice a break in the logs of 48 minutes and 54 seconds," Blith replied. "And this is important: remember the internal systems clock will show *our* time, not yours."

He had a faraway look on his face. "I never could have imagined coming back here to provide closure," he said, feeling choked up. "Let alone that Ozma and Chatulah were destined to meet each other."

"I know," Arial answered softly. "And speaking of Chatulah," she handed him the picture, "she wanted me to give this to you and eventually Ozma." He unfolded the picture and noticed some hand-written Hebrew on it; the date was 10th of Adar 5805. "*Yehonatan*," Arial whispered with a few tears, "it says 'forgiven' - in Chatulah's own hand."

"Oh wow," was all that he could say. "Okay, I'll keep it in the inner pocket on my suit." He tucked it in safe. "And Arial?"

"Yes, *Yehonatan*?"

"I think it was wonderful that you and Kyle found each other." He noticed Arial's blushing.

Blith lightly ribbed her. "Yeah, they really were in love!"

Politely laughing, he attached his helmet, air hoses, and gloves. He felt a tap on his helmet and turned towards the two women. "Those satellites also have a ten-megapixel camera - good for weather observation," Arial informed him and Blith joked about her being a geek!

"Arial," she protested, "they would have found that out eventually."

Jonathan just grinned. "I'm certain we'll find a use for that, Arial," he assured her, receiving Arial's pleased look.

Relaxing, he said, "Now for the other."

Ozma and Chatulah

Ozma had enjoyed the impromptu dancing that she, Chatulah, and the remaining crew of the *Golda Meir* had performed to "Hava Nagila" by Andre Rieu. At long last, she had been able to compare her long hair with the rest as they swayed and frolicked in zero-gravity.

However, it was time. She clung to her helmet while Chatulah floated in front of her. Both had faint tears in their eyes and Ozma had a lump in her throat. "I'm sorry that I wasn't the best help you could have had," she said while fighting back her emotions.

Chatulah, however, only smiled and placed her hands on Ozma's shoulders. "No, Ozma," she confessed. "*You* were the very person I needed."

Touched, Ozma clasped Chatulah's hands. "Thank you," She managed to get out. "I..."

"Ozma, we are both changed. I shall always remember you, my dear friend."

Ozma leaned in and so did Chatulah; they hugged tightly. "Before you go," Chatulah whispered, "my name is...Tamar."

Ozma's face glowed with appreciation. "Such a sweet and beautiful name!"

"Thank you. And now, you must return to Oz." Chatulah took Ozma's helmet and attached it to her suit. A final sniffle, and Ozma headed to the hatch leading to the upper bay. She waved at Chatulah as she closed the hatch behind her and then floated upward, using little handrails to pull herself along.

Aleichem Shalom, Ozma and *Yehonatan*

He watched as Blith and Arial guided Ozma along to the passenger's seat and secured her in, the gloves and air hoses connected. Blith then secured the hatch near Ozma. Johnathan watched her float around until she rejoined Arial on his side.

"*Shalom*, Arial and Blith." He held out his hand to be held by theirs.

"*Aleichem Shalom*, Ozma and *Yehonatan*!" both women declared, and Arial then secured his hatch. He observed them enter the tunnel and the last hatch close behind them.

The upper bay doors opened. The Bravo's display confirmed the movements through an animated sequence, portraying an image of the Bravo with the booster. Finally, they were clear of both the bay and the *Golda Meir* and the Bravo was maneuvered to point directly towards the wormhole.

"BOOSTER COUNTDOWN," the cockpit display flashed.

"Let's go home, Ozma." Jonathan grabbed her gloves and she squeezed back, smiling the widest he had ever seen.

"5...4...3...2...1...IGNITION!" And they were off. Their speed kept increasing and increasing, and the time left to enter the wormhole counted backwards. "BOOSTER SEPARATION! 3...2...1..." The wormhole grew larger and larger.

"Here we go, Ozma!" Jonathan announced, but noticed Ozma had fallen asleep! "That's a switch," he joked.

"20 SECONDS TO WORMHOLE," the display announced.

Johnathan smiled and then nearly slapped his helmet. "You big dummy! I need to make this all as similar to before we entered." He quickly grabbed Ozma's gloves as well as his and stowed them away. The helmets came off next and were secured where they had been before. He took his flight tablet and stuck it to the center console –

the Velcro held it fast. His eyes were becoming heavy and he disconnected their air hoses. Johnathan barely managed to loosen Ozma's belts up an inch before he too fell asleep.

Then the Bravo penetrated the wormhole.

A New Future

Chatulah and Aitan were alone in the cockpit of the *Golda Meir*. Both silently observed the Bravo enter the wormhole and then simply waited. After nearly two minutes, the wormhole closed up on itself. Aitan just watched Chatulah, who only sniffled.

"What now, Chatulah?" he politely inquired.

She only sighed in response.

"You forgave her."

She nodded with a faraway look.

"Something from Paul Boese comes to mind, Chatulah, and I think it's perfect for this: 'forgiveness does not change the past, but it does enlarge the future'." His voice was soft. "You were the only one who believed your great-grandmother, and you swore to her on her deathbed to avenge her and her people. You were vindicated—the stories were indeed all true—and you really did meet the 'One'."

He gave her a little cloth so she could wipe her eyes. After several deep breaths, she finally spoke up. "After the Garden, she told me that every night she had had nightmares of what our people went through - I saw her react to the one about the Twins and Mengele. She told me that a 'still, small voice' would tell her to 'ask for her forgiveness'."

"At this point in time, you were both brought together - one needed to ask for forgiveness and the other needed to forgive."

"Yes, and strangely enough, by giving I was also set free."

"Very true, Chatulah. Forgiveness can be a harsh, yet healing medicine," he agreed. "So, what now, Chatulah?" he repeated, and she stayed quiet for nearly a minute.

Taking his hands, she smiled. "Tamar. Just call me by my real name."

The beginning.

14ᵀᴴ OF IYAR, 5807
(FRIDAY, 10 MAY 2047)
EPILOGUE

S.R.E.S.S. *HALEY (SRV-1972) MUSEUM DEDICATION PATRIOTS POINT, MOUNT PLEASANT SOUTH CAROLINA*

It was a pleasant spring day in the Lowcountry of South Carolina. A slight drizzle was the only obstacle to enjoying an otherwise perfect day – especially for the dedication ceremony of the *Haley* Museum. Abana stood with Abira and two other gentlemen while Arial was a distance away at Kyle DeLeon's grave. The rest of the *Golda Meir* crew was already in the museum; today's festivities would be their last official act as members of Crew 4.

Abana turned to the first gentleman – a man of average build with blue eyes, black hair, and glasses. His left knee sported a brace from a recent ACL reconstruction surgery – compliments of an accident during a pickup flag-football game. He donned a pressed blue flight suit with tunic and the gray flight beret; his boots held a high shine. "Captain Jon Kryton," Abana said, "congratulations on your promotion." And then she joked, "It looks like you celebrated a little too much!"

"Much appreciated, Abana," Jon replied. "I had been looking forward to returning to spaceflight duty since my stint as the Department Head of the SRSEC's Spacecraft Recovery Branch. My family says it's a blessing in disguise. Perhaps next year."

"I can imagine you really wouldn't have wanted to miss this event though?" Abana inquired.

"No," Jon answered. "I was among the first to read the email from your government and the ISA. It's enough that you and the *Golda Meir* returned the *Haley's* original Bravo. For now, my suggestions still stand."

"I agree, Jon. It's all in the hands of the politicians," Abana concurred and then glanced at the man next to Jon – a bearish figure with glasses, a goatee, and a mustache. He wore a stylish gray fedora with a black hatband. Rounding out his clothes were a green polo shirt, black slacks, and comfortable black leather shoes. At his side was a perpetually smiling Welsh Pembroke Corgi dog – the stubby tail shook with a blur. "And now, who is this fine gentleman and his happy dog?" Abana wished to know.

"Abana and Abira, it's my pleasure to introduce to you Mr. Alex Byron and his support dog Ziggy. Alex is our official historian for the SRSEC and he is fully cleared with the need-to-know for the discussion after the festivities," Jon explained and Ziggy responded with a "*ra-roo*!" Corgi salutation.

"I am very pleased to meet y'all," Alex said with a strong southern drawl. "And I assure you ladies, everything in that meeting will be entirely...off the record."

Abana smiled and so did her XO. They resumed watching Arial off in the distance. "She is paying her respects," she informed the two men. "I can imagine she's also talking about the status of the *Haley's* survivors."

"That reminds me," Alex brought up, "the Bravo that returned through the wormhole – what would any of you have given to have been in that third seat?"

Both Abana and Abira laughed politely. "It took everything we had to not follow them in!" Abana conveyed. "My Chief Engineer said we weren't meant to go – leave it to the Rabbis, she said."

"Good answer," Jon quipped. "Would you have wanted to go, Alex?"

"As long as Ziggy would be with me," Alex cheerfully responded. Ziggy gave him many licks in appreciation.

"Of course!" Abana said approvingly. "We did see the image of the planet on the other side of the wormhole."

"That had to have been something else," Alex commented.

"It was," Abira answered. "Seeing the wormhole was the highlight of my career."

"Knowing what happened to them—and at least knowing that two of them are still alive—is what made mine." Abana spoke and the four became quiet. Finally, she started to walk towards Arial. "I shall get her."

Arial's Respects

She had been whispering the entire time. "Oh, my beloved. I have so longed to be with you. I have thought of you every day since you passed. Me and the rest of the *Golda Meir* are here to dedicate a museum to your ship - the *Haley*. Dearest, we recovered their Bravo!" She teared up and knelt by his grave. "And though the world cannot know the full truth, I will tell you. David and Jonathan, they're still alive in a world of unbelievable wonders! David has a new wife and she is so beautiful!"

Arial felt a gentle tap and seeing that it was Abana, she finished. "But Jonathan—oh my sweetest Kyle—Jonathan has not only a wonderful new wife, but a wholly new adopted family! One of his daughters is from India and she is so precious, my lovely. I have to go now, but I wanted to tell you how much I still love you and one day we'll explore the stars together. Perhaps maybe we'll join them in that magical land!"

She then took a red rose, kissed its petals, and laid it on his headstone. Arm in arm with Abana, she walked back, smiling with a relieved and contented heart.

ABOUT THE AUTHOR

James Walter (J.W.) Krych had his first novel, *From Neptune to Earth*, as a collaborative work between him and David Cuciz, a member of the Swiss Army at the time. *The Flight to Oz Book I: Arrival* was his first-ever Science Fiction/Fantasy story based on the characters and world of L. Frank Baum's *Wizard of Oz* series. *The Flight to Oz Book II: Anusha of Oz* was a direct sequel to *Book I* and included a new Original Character with Asperger's Syndrome. *This Point in Time* is the first book based on his *Flight to Oz* universe and deals with the Holocaust and forgiveness. Starting in 1988, James served in the US Military finally retiring as a CW2 in 2011. As a Warrant Officer, he was first assigned to the Joint Force Headquarters in Columbus, Ohio, preparing for natural and/or man-made disasters. Relocating to South Carolina, he became a member of the 218th MEB and finished his last two years of service on active duty orders as the Brigade S-6 IT Signal Warrant Officer for the CCMRF, the CBRNE (Chemical, Biological, Radiological, Nuclear and Explosives) Consequence Management Response Force, Mission, where circumstances would have had to be terribly bad in order to be called up. He and his wife, Lori, and their two special-needs boys live in the Charleston, SC, area, along with their cats. He can be reached on Deviant Art: http://centurion030.deviantart.com/ and on Facebook: https://www.facebook.com/TheFlightToOz

Made in United States
North Haven, CT
22 April 2022